TRAIL BOSS

BERNARD PALMER

LIVING BOOKS
Tyndale House Publishers, Inc.
Wheaton, Illinois

First printing, November 1986

Library of Congress Catalog Card Number 86-50746
ISBN 0-8423-7308-X

1

John Breckenridge gathered the reins in his powerful young hand and swung into the saddle. Briefly he squinted over the backs of the mindless, ever-moving crush of longhorns. The grass had been grazed short the past few days and sharp hooves were beginning to cut it off at the roots, pulverizing the hard soil and raising little puffs of dust around constantly restless feet. The cattle should have been started north two weeks before. Trying to hold them on poor grass could be disastrous.

John had already seen one near-stampede that day with forty head escaping to hide in the brakes. They could explode again at the slightest provocation.

Both cattle and men were uneasy. Tempers were short, and impending trouble, like a cloud, hung apprehensively over them.

He turned the rump of his Morgan gelding to the dying sun. With a feather-light touch he booted his mount away from the fretful, lowing longhorns at a brisk canter. The cut on his cheek where a bulky fist caught him two hours before had stopped bleeding but turned a livid purple. The bandage that covered the slash in his upper arm bulged under his shirt sleeve. Cookie had cleaned out the knife wound after the fight and disinfected it.

John ignored the throbbing of his arm and forced his attention to the task ahead. The jerry-built frontier town was eight miles away. It would be dark before he got there, but that didn't matter. Kramer and his sidekick would still be in the saloon, slouched over the bar or the faro table.

Anger glinted in John's pale gray eyes. Kramer didn't deserve to have a herd. Every hand on the drive resented his leaving. The cattle were restive and irritable. It was a difficult time and the drovers needed all the help they could get. But Kramer had gone to town, taking a crony with him. That meant there were two less to help if trouble exploded.

Breckenridge knew why he found reason to leave. They were faced with a long, dangerous trek that would take months to complete and could well end with the deaths of some of his men. It was tempting to have one last bout at the bar and the gaming table.

John scarcely knew the man he had thrown in with. He had learned that Kramer was taking a herd north and sought him out. John had three hundred fifty head of his own, bought with a small stake of gold he had panned in the mountains of Colorado. He only had two drovers—not enough to take even so small a herd all the way to Montana. He had been looking for someone to throw in with but had been unsuccessful until he heard about Kramer. It was not a situation to his liking, but it was getting late in the season and to wait longer would be to risk the early snows.

Kramer was granite-hard. And the chances

6

were that he had used a long rope and a running iron to build his herd. Yet he knew the trail, he knew cattle, and he was good with a gun. Breckenridge was satisfied with his decision until that morning when his partner called him aside and said he was taking one of the men and going to town.

"So, you'll be in charge until we get back."

John's gray eyes hardened. "This is no time for celebrating."

The older man's cheeks flushed and anger curled his thin lips. "Who said anything about celebrating?"

"That's why you're going to town, ain't it?"

"That's none of your business."

The cowhand's eyes narrowed. "The grass is about gone and so is the water. If we don't get cracking, those longhorns ain't going to be in shape to start a drive."

"We'll move out when I get good and ready. Not before!"

"The men are jumpy and so are those mean-tempered critters they'll be driving," Breckenridge persisted. "It's not going to take a whole lot to set them off."

The trail boss glared at him. "If you can't handle them, I'll find somebody who can."

The corners of John's mouth tightened. "I just don't like asking for trouble."

Kramer's voice raised above the lowing of the cattle and the unmelodious singing of the men on the line. "If you aren't satisfied with the way I run this outfit, cut out those beeves of yours and go it alone!"

John wanted to do just that. But going it alone with two men would be a disaster—even worse than putting up with Kramer. "We made a deal," he said. "I'm staying by it."

Kramer turned and called over his shoulder to the drover who would be going with him. "Come on, Jake. Let's ride."

Breckenridge watched apprehensively as Kramer and Jake rode off. It wasn't going to be easy to hold the men in line if they got their backs up.

Although John anticipated problems and kept a wary eye out for the first sight of trouble, everything would have gone smoothly had the boss come back that night. But darkness wore on and he did not show.

Morning broke cold and clear with dew on the grass and thin wisps of fog lying in the lowlands. The sun still hid below the eastern horizon but darkness was giving way to daylight. Long gray fingers stretched across the plains to reveal the forms of greasewood and tender green tumbleweeds beginning to take shape after the spring rains. The wind stirred from its night of slumber, whipping one corner of the canvas fly that was stretched over the rear of the chuck wagon and the table to provide shade and a bit of shelter for the cook. The sudden movement spooked a horse. He shied and crow-hopped over the rough ground, almost piling his unsuspecting rider into a clump of yucca.

A mule cow jerked up her head, eyes rolling in terror. She snorted wildly. Instantly a dozen longhorns began to move, bellowing their fears. Horns clanked against each other and the cattle surged forward. Only the quick action of the drovers turned them back.

"Better tie that canvas down, Cookie," John

ordered. "You know what that flapping can do to a bunch of nervous critters."

"They're apt to spook anyway," Cookie grumbled as he retied the canvas shelter. "That ornery batch of walkin' beefsteaks is mighty uneasy. They're apt to take off any minute."

John stood in the stirrups and surveyed the restless mass before him.

That decided him. He was going to move the cattle to better grass and water some distance up the arroyo. The change would only be good for a few days, but it would give them a little more time.

He sought out the drovers who were having breakfast and told them to start the herd to fresh grass as soon as they relieved the night men.

"Kramer ain't goin' to like that," a hard-featured hand by the name of Gilson countered belligerently. "He don't want no cattle of his moved without his say-so."

"When you're in charge, Gilson, you can do as you please. Right now I'm ramrodding this outfit."

John waited, eyes searching the faces of the men squatting around the fire. He expected Gilson to challenge him, but he only glared in silence.

Breakfast was over for the first shift and they were riding out to relieve the night crew when a sudden burst of wind whipped the hat from a drover's head and sent it spinning eerily in the direction of the herd. It slammed against a walleyed old bull, and he exploded into a wild, headlong run. A surging mass of steers, bulls, and mule cows charged after him, snorting and blowing in terror.

John Breckenridge spurred his mount, risking the thrust of sword-sharp horns in a frantic effort

9

to cut off the stampeding cattle from the rest of the herd before they joined the wild rush. He was flanked by two quick-thinking drovers, as courageous and reckless as himself. They shouted above the din, beating the longhorns about the head with their wide-brimmed hats in a frantic effort to turn the herd in against itself.

The cattle dashed on but there was still a measure of uncertainty in their movements. That uncertainty gave the drovers time to act. Cutting off the critters that had bolted from the main herd, the riders pressed the outer rim in against the others. Like a whirlpool in a fast-moving river they swept around. The sounds of clattering horns punctuated the thunder of hooves and the yells of the drovers. The movement of the cattle fed on itself, picking up momentum as the noise and confusion increased in intensity.

The instant the herd's forward motion stopped, John again forced his mount in among the milling longhorns. Deftly he cut out fifteen head, forcing them from the churning mass. Three other hands did the same and the rest circled the herd, singing loudly to assure the frightened animals that all was well. Minutes passed and they cut out another batch, then another and another. Gradually the turning movement halted.

The cattle were still uneasy and the situation was dangerous, but the immediate peril eased. Vigilance on the part of the drovers could keep the herd contained if nothing else happened. John stared across the prairie, scarcely noting the rider who came up beside him.

Saddle leather creaked as a drover rode up. "Want me to take a couple of the boys and go after those mavericks?"

John shook his head. "We're going to move the herd first and be sure they're quieted."

The drover shrugged indifferently.

By this time the hands had started the longhorns north. Cookie had packed up the chuck wagon and had taken off with the wrangler moving the remuda some distance to one side. John should have been leading the long procession, but they weren't going far and the cattle were so edgy he had to be certain everything was in order. He rode beside the drovers on point for a time. Theirs was the primary responsibility, and the most experienced hands had been chosen for that position. They held the herd to a slow, measured walk, taking care not to move suddenly or make any unnecessary noise. Fortunately the men at swing and flank were seasoned drovers as well, used to the ways of the herd and veterans of all too many stampedes. They knew exactly what had to be done and how to do it.

Breckenridge relaxed slightly. The situation was still dangerous. It wouldn't take much to set them off again. A covey of quail exploding noisily from a clump of greasewood or mesquite; the sudden, thoughtless movement of a rider or horse; or the chilling buzz of a diamondback rattler would do it.

But the moving had a quieting effect. The longhorns found reassurance and comfort in doing the bidding of the drovers. They still tensed, shivering at the slightest sound, but they were content to plod north.

He was only taking them two miles to another feeding ground—a distance so short the herd scarcely had time to form properly. Yet he kept a close watch. He reined in and allowed the nervous

11

longhorns to move by him, taking note of the hands who were working them. Those riding drag were the least experienced, but even in hiring for that position Kramer had used caution—another indication that he knew cattle and the men who handled them.

The drovers were constantly on the move, turning back those critters that might have strayed and keeping the herd tightly bunched. They approached the new grazing grounds without incident.

Now that the cattle were on good grass, Cookie prepared the noon meal. John Breckenridge stayed on the line while half of the drovers ate and only went in when they returned to take over. If all went well they could start beating the arroyos for strays the next morning. John was lingering over a second cup of coffee with Cookie when two grizzled hands sidled away from the campfire in the direction of the remuda. He recognized them immediately. The gaunt, wiry Gilson had challenged his authority. The other was Bull Murray, a massive brute who was constantly at Gilson's side.

"Sending those two after the boss?" Cookie wanted to know.

"I'm not sending anybody anywhere."

Cookie glanced crookedly at John out of watery, half-closed eyes. He was a strange man, garrulous one moment and silent and moody the next. When he was talkative his mouth was going constantly. Everything he saw, everything anyone said, reminded him of a long, detailed story that captured the attention of his audience. But when he was in one of those morose moods he wrapped himself in silence, and woe to the one

12

who violated it. He had few friends, but still fewer enemies.

Cookie was just there, a fixture on the drive like the yellow slickers and chaps of the drovers. Men did not grow close to him. It was as easy to buddy up to a saddle blanket or a pair of hobbles. But he could put out a good meal and on occasion he could tell an interesting yarn. That afternoon was one of those rare occasions when all had gone well and Cookie was open and expansive. He watched the two riders slip from the fire to the remuda.

"Maybe you ain't sending Gilson and Murray anywhere," the cook said, "but they're sure as shootin' on their way."

John's forehead crinkled. He drained the last drops of coffee from his cup, got to his feet, and set it on the improvised table.

"Be careful," the cook warned under his breath. "You can't trust those two buzzards any more than you can a rattlesnake. Especially when they're together."

John moved forward as though he had not heard the whispered words of caution, but his mind registered all that was said. He had read the same warning in the manner of Gilson and Murray—the look of a slinking coyote sparring for an advantage before he attacked.

"The skinny guy's the dangerous one," Cookie continued. "You keep a close watch on him."

John's boots crunched noisily on the hard sod as he approached the two drovers. They heard him and faced him, hostility gleaming in their taut features.

Bull Murray swore. He was taller than Gilson

13

by a head, at least twenty pounds heavier and as powerfully built as a he-grizzly. His nose had been badly broken at least twice, knocked askew in long-forgotten fights. An ear had been crumpled and thickened along the top by some adversary's fist and his left eye drooped permanently. One corner of his mouth was drawn down in a perpetual sneer.

"Where do you think you're going?" John asked.

"That's none of your business!"

"If you want to ride for this outfit, it is."

Murray moved a step closer, his hamlike fist cocked ominously. "Did I hear you right?" he blustered.

"It depends on what you heard!"

"It's none of your business what Gilson and I do."

"You know the orders. No one leaves camp until Kramer gets back."

"That so?" The huge drover's thick lips twisted into an evil grin. "I never heard him say anything about that."

"You heard me."

Murray laughed.

John moved closer in easy, catlike steps. "I don't want to have trouble with you."

The big man leaned forward, a snarl twisting his features. "Nobody wants trouble with me!"

"You don't have to worry about what Kramer'll do for letting us go to town," Gilson broke in. "We know him better than anybody. We fought in the war with him. He's not going to send you packing for not stopping us. When we see him we'll fix everything."

"I don't need anybody to fix anything,"

14

Breckenridge repeated, his voice ominously quiet and devoid of emotion. "You aren't going to town or anywhere else."

For the first time Murray realized he was facing a man who was not afraid of him—one who was not quaking at the prospect of having to fight him. Murray was a simple, direct individual who did not see ahead. He took one thing at a time, feet planted firmly on the ground and fists at the ready. He waited momentarily, sizing this new opponent.

"Gilson can do what you say if he wants to. That's up to him!" he roared. "But you aren't telling me what to do!"

"Then go get your gear and ride."

Bull snorted angrily. "Kramer hired us! He'll have to fire us! . . . Now, turn yourself around and go about your business before I lose my temper!"

2

John balanced lightly on the balls of his feet and Murray crouched a few feet away. The big man's breathing was fast and shallow, and the cunning in those pale blue eyes warned that he would strike when he had the advantage. He was disagreeable as a polecat, but completely predictable.

Like Cookie said, however, Gilson was the more dangerous of the two, the one to watch— nimble on his feet and lightning fast. He was a patient, crafty fighter, content to stand back for Murray to launch the attack. And while he waited, his sharp eyes searched for that little chink in John's defense—for the split instant his guard might drop or his attention be distracted.

Breckenridge would have to do battle with both of them, but with Murray first. And a battle it would be. The powerful drover was not used to defeat. At the same time he would not be able to forget Gilson or allow him out of his line of vision. To do so would be disastrous.

"Scared?" John baited, a thin, mirthless smile warping his features.

That was more than Murray could stand. Bawling his rage he waded toward John. Pushing close he threw a powerful, looping fist that was calculated to crush John's defense and explode on his jaw. But Breckenridge expected just such an attack. He saw the swing coming and rolled to one side, avoiding the blow. In that same fluid motion John unleashed a short, wicked jab that caught his opponent on the side of the head, snapping his head to one side.

The blow was completely unexpected. Murray staggered under the force of it and almost went down. He caught himself on one knee, balanced there with a hand on the hard turf. He shook his head stupidly. John danced backwards, his huge fists knotted to strike again. The bigger man got the cobwebs out of his head and managed to stand. Flat-footed, he stared at his opponent. Then he moved slowly out of the crouch and inched toward John with more caution than he had shown until that moment. His overconfidence had been hammered away by that powerful left. But he was still as cunning and unpredictable as a cornered wolf—and far more dangerous.

Breckenridge was as strong as Bull and familiar with the technique of boxing. He feinted, found an opening, and drove a sledgehammer fist through Murray's guard to send him reeling. Every move was accomplished with confidence and bewildering speed and skill. It was difficult for the drover to land a solid, decisive blow.

But Murray was not beaten yet. The big drover had never backed away in a fight. He battled by instinct, his massive strength honed by a hundred bitter frontier confrontations. He had gouged the eye out of one man unfortunate enough to do battle with him and had bitten the ear off another. His reputation had spread far. Wherever men gossiped around the campfires or in saloons they talked about him.

John waited for an opening. When it came he lashed out with the blinding speed of a rattler. His powerful fists slammed into Bull in quick succession—a right followed closely by a devastating left. The blows blurred the big man's vision and staggered him. He slowed Murray but the drover continued to move in. He was not lacking in courage but didn't have the speed to avoid being caught by those hamlike fists.

John pounded him relentlessly with savage, stinging blows that rocked him back on his heels. Bull swayed uncertainly and forgot all about trying to match John's technique. Roaring, he lowered his head and charged, throwing a wild right that would have ended the fight with a less skillful man. But Breckenridge saw it coming. Nimbly he bobbed to one side, jerking his head just enough to allow the huge fist to graze his cheek bone. It cut a livid path that flamed red behind Murray's knuckles. The punch threw Murray off balance. Before he could get set again John whipped a blistering right to the face. It drove past Bull's defenses to catch him full on the bridge of his nose.

Blood spurted and he lurched frantically backward and to one side. By this time his nose was broken again and there was a deep cut on his chin. Blood stained his whiskers. His ear was swollen and turning purple, and he rocked on his heels.

Crablike, he spread his arms and waited just beyond John's reach. As Breckenridge danced closer, Bull ducked a jab and rushed in, encircling his waist with a powerful bear hug. He lifted the gangling cowhand from his feet and would have crashed him to the ground, but John managed to get his arms up, forcing them against the big man's chest. Thrusting himself away from his burly assailant, he butted Murray viciously in the face with his head. A cut opened over one eye and blood spurted. The sudden pain caused the drover to relax his viselike grip. Breckenridge shoved him away so brutally he went down and for a moment stayed there numbly, shaking his head.

Gilson, who had remained out of the fray until that moment, jerked a Green River Buffalo Skinner from his boot and moved in. He brandished the wicked, slightly curved blade. It was a knife made for utilitarian purposes but, honed to razor sharpness, it was a formidable weapon. He moved closer, cautiously, staying just beyond the reach of John's knotted fists, crafty as an old lobo wolf circling for the kill. He was quicker and smarter and far more dangerous than his massive, slow-witted companion.

By this time Murray's head cleared. He scrambled to his feet and took up the fight again.

Breckenridge backed against a clump of mesquite to give himself a measure of protection from the rear and the sides. Warily he studied his adversaries. He was in a precarious situation.

Murray slogged close and slammed a blow to John's stomach. The pain was sharp and Breckenridge gasped for breath. Eager for the kill, Bull waded closer, but the tall, broad-shouldered young cowhand was not finished yet. He ducked away from the roundhouse.

Gilson had been darting in, pretending to strike, and dancing back in an effort to keep John off balance. Now, however, holding the knife shoulder high, he lunged forward, determined to finish him. John anticipated the move and kicked savagely, catching the would-be knifer on the shin bone just below the knee. Gilson cried out in pain and his grip on the knife relaxed.

That was the opening Breckenridge had been waiting for. He sank a powerful blow to Murray's belly, his fist burying itself in the soft flesh just above the belt buckle. The big man grunted and staggered back, eyes glazed and defenses dropped. John wrapped his big arms around him, turned and hurtled him backwards into Gilson. They both collapsed on the grass.

This sudden and devastating move gave Breckenridge the advantage. He clawed his heavy hog-leg from its holster in one swift motion and brought it to bear on them before they could scramble to their feet.

"Stay where you are!" he rasped. "Don't make another move! Either of you!"

"Put that thing away!" Gilson said plaintively. "Can't you take a little funnin'?"

"Toss your knife over here real careful like," he grated. "I just might get the idea you're going to throw it and pull the trigger."

"We've got no quarrel with you," Bull Murray muttered.

"That's not the way you were acting." John was still breathing heavily.

"We didn't figure on doing anything," Gilson whined. "You ought to know that."

His expression did not change. "You pulled a knife and that plumb riled me. Now, toss it here! And be quick about it!"

Gilson did as he was told and Breckenridge moved forward, stooping to pick it up without taking his eyes from the two men.

"Now, can we get up?" Bull demanded, a whine creeping into his tone.

20

"Stay where you are!"

By this time the color had returned to their cheeks.

"You wouldn't shoot!" Gilson blustered.

"Try me."

"Take your finger off the trigger," Murray pleaded, even more desperate than before. "We don't want no trouble."

John laughed, his eyes as bleak and cold as January in Montana. "You've got a funny way of showin' it."

3

John disarmed Gilson and Murray and backed over to their saddled mounts, keeping a wary eye on both of them. He jerked their rifles from their holsters and threw them on the ground.

"Now, get out of here!"

"You wouldn't be so high and mighty if you knew how close we are to Kramer," Gilson muttered. "You'll be in big trouble when he finds out."

"It won't be any trouble I can't handle."

"We're friends of Kramer's from way back," Murray blustered. "Fought the war together!"

"You better listen to what Bull's a-tellin' you," his companion put in. "Kramer takes care of his friends."

Fire gleamed in John's pale gray eyes. "I'm sick of you both! Get out of here!"

Murray rubbed his cheek tenderly. "You can't run us off! We ain't been paid yet."

"Kramer's in town," Breckenridge said, his voice iced. "Talk to him about it."

"What about our guns?"

"Talk to Kramer about them, too."

They stepped onto their horses. "We'll be back!" Gilson grated softly. "You'll pay for what you done today." With that he booted his mount and galloped off. Murray followed reluctantly.

Cookie was at the chuck wagon, a grin splitting his whiskered face. "That was a long time coming," he said. "They've been asking for trouble ever since they hired on."

Breckenridge went to the campfire and squatted close enough to feel the warmth of the coals, rubbing his bruised face with his hand.

It was then that Cookie noticed blood oozing from a slash in his upper arm. "Looks like Gilson got you with his knife. Get that shirt off. We'll have to clean up the cut and stop the bleeding."

John followed him to the wagon and peeled off his shirt. Cookie washed the wound with clean, soapy water, disinfected it with whiskey, and bound it tightly.

"Want a swig?"

"No, thanks. Never touch the stuff."

"Wish I could say the same." Cookie tilted the bottle and took a long pull at it. "It's plumb near ruined me."

"Kramer's given orders. There's to be no liquor in camp."

Cookie grinned. "I ain't got any whiskey. Just medicine."

He put the bottle away. "You were plumb lucky. When Gilson whipped out that buffalo skinner I thought you'd get your everlasting."

John stared glumly into the dying embers. He had the cattle to think about. They appeared to be calm enough but he was shorthanded by four now. If they stayed quiet, there would be no problems, but he had long since learned not to take such things for granted. It would be safe only to expect the worst, to consider each possibility as though it was sure to happen. And that meant hiring new men.

He had no choice. He had to go to town, get Kramer out of the saloon and convince him that new hands were needed to help round up the strays and get the herd moving. First, however, he had to satisfy himself that all was well. He saddled the Morgan gelding and circled the cattle carefully, searching for signs of unrest or probable trouble. Satisfied that all was well, John rode up to one of the more reliable drovers and put him in charge.

"Kramer ain't going to like it having you traipse into town after him," the hand said laconically.

"I can't help that."

By this time the sun was low on the horizon and a gentle spring breeze was picking up. It was quiet, save for the meadowlarks singing their joy of living and the occasional yipping of a coyote in the distance. Long afternoon shadows reached out from an occasional clump of mesquite and greasewood and cactus, tracing strange shapes along the prairie. It was hard to believe there could be trouble at such a time.

One of the drovers, crossing in front of Breckenridge, waved to him. John swung his gelding and loped off in the direction of the Texas town. With the disappearance of daylight, the wind died and a breathless hush settled over the prairie. Darkness unfolded and the moon poked its silvery face above the horizon, silhouetting a lone wolf trotting purposefully along the ridge to the rider's left. The night's hunt was just beginning. And from the arroyo on the other side an owl mournfully wailed its loneliness.

The black John rode was a powerful animal, bred for the wide prairies and sparse water holes

24

and dry creeks. This horse could carry a rider all day without rest and little water and still summon strength to keep moving from some inner reservoir.

The night was still young when John rode into the little Texas town. He approached the squalid assortment of adobe and clapboard buildings scattered haphazardly along either side of the wide street, making his way past the blacksmith's shop and the general store that also housed the post office. Across the way someone had built a home close to the two-story frame hotel, mute evidence that the builder had not expected the town to grow beyond its present business district. Up the street he could make out one of the bigger saloons with a dozen horses at the hitching rail.

He made for it with the confidence of one long familiar with the weaknesses and follies of man. As he neared the long, ramshackle building he saw that the horses he expected were not tied there. But that did not mean the two men were not in the saloon. Kramer, for all of his faults, was one to take care of his horse. They had been in town for two days. The animals would be in the livery stable, properly fed and watered.

John stopped at the far end of the rail and tied his own mount with a slipknot that would come free in an instant in case he had to leave in a hurry.

The horses Murray and Gilson had ridden out of camp were there, which was about what he had expected. They would have gone straight to Kramer. He paused, loosened his weapon in its holster, and once more started forward.

They couldn't have known he would come into town so the chances were slim that they would be outside waiting for him. Still, he could not be sure. Hiding in a place where they could get a bullet in his back was their style. His keen gray eyes missed nothing. Men died because they made the mistake of assuming they knew what an enemy might do.

He paused outside the swinging doors. Then he straightened and stepped inside, surveying the smoky, dimly-lighted room. A dozen men bellied up to the bar, and almost that many more were seated around the battered tables. The bartender, eyes bloodshot from lack of sleep and the smoke that hung in a thick blue haze around the kerosene lamps, mechanically replenished the drinks of the men in front of him. A waiter, his ample waist encompassed by a grubby apron, padded wearily from table to bar and back again.

In the far corner a player piano hammered out an off-key tune, almost drowned by the continuous hum of many voices. The hour was still early but a number of the customers had been long at the bottle. Their tongues were loose, their voices loud and belligerent.

Squinting against the smoke, Breckenridge searched the place but saw no sign of Kramer and his companions. He took two steps forward, peering intently at the tables. Satisfied at last that they were not in the saloon he moved to the end of the bar and leaned on it, his back to the bartender.

"Looking for somebody?" a gravelly voice behind him asked.

He turned toward the bartender. "I thought a guy I know would be here. A big character—a cattleman—with a walrus mustache and a powerful thirst."

The bartender dried the glass in his hand and returned it to the shelf along the back wall. "I've seen him. What are you wanting him for?"

John's eyes narrowed. "It's a private matter."

The bartender recognized the tone. "It doesn't mean anything to me, one way or the other. You don't need to get your back up."

John stared once more at the unfamiliar faces seated at the tables and the grimy, unshaven lot along the bar. "Happen to know where I can find him?"

The lanky saloon keeper finished waiting on a customer before answering. "Yep."

Breckenridge waited for him to continue.

"He's over at the jail house. The sheriff's got him and those sidekicks of his locked up."

"What did they do? Try to tear the place apart?"

"You might say that." A customer who had already had too much to drink called for another bottle. Mechanically the barkeeper took one from the shelf behind him and set it on the bar. "But I can't say as I blame him. I'd have been a mite upset myself if I'd just lost my herd."

Breckenridge sucked in his breath sharply. "How's that again?"

"He lost his herd playing faro. The whole shooting match!"

4

John's lithe frame stiffened. "It must've been some game!"

"He and that sidekick of his started playing faro with Rafferty last night. Sam's the gambler here. The skinny guy didn't last too long. He ran out of money."

"That would be Jake Norris."

"Anyway, he tried to get the big guy to quit, but Kramer—I guess that's his handle—kept right on playing and right on losing. They played most of the night till I closed them down. I thought maybe that would be the end of it, but they were back this morning. The big guy kept saying Rafferty had to stay with him and give him a chance to win his money back."

"It must not've worked that way."

"And that's the pure truth. They played all day and were still at it when two other guys joined them. Looked like they'd been on the wrong end of a fight. They started drinking like they wanted to run us dry and tried to tell the big guy what somebody had done to them, but he wasn't listening. His bad luck kept right on. First thing you know, Kramer put up the title to his herd and . . ." The bartender shrugged. "And he wasn't as lucky at faro as he thought. He lost it all. The whole kit and caboodle."

John frowned. "Reckon I'll have to go over to the jail house to talk to him."

"In case you don't know where the jail is, it's up the street a ways." He gestured vaguely with a soft white hand. "Between the courthouse and the undertaker's on the west side of the street. You can't miss it."

Breckenridge pushed past the swinging doors into the fresh night air. On the boardwalk he paused until his eyes grew accustomed to the darkness. The din coming from the building behind him was a jarring, discordant jumble of sound. No one else was in sight, and save for the horses at the rail in front of the saloon he could see nothing.

He could not have missed the jail. The courthouse, a large adobe structure, presented an imposing spectacle just beyond the row of store buildings. The undertaker's parlor was across the street on the next corner and the jail house was located between them. It, too, was a squat adobe building with bars in the windows and a heavy oak door guarding the opening to the little office.

Breckenridge could see the sheriff hunched over the desk, his lean features silhouetted by the kerosene lamp. The cowhand tied his mount to the post outside and approached the building. The sound of his spurs and footsteps alerted the officer.

"Looking for someone?"

"I need answers more than anything else." He lowered his big frame into a battered captain's chair and crossed his legs. "Then I might want to see those prisoners you picked up over at the saloon."

"It won't do you any good to see them tonight," the sheriff replied. "They were roaring drunk when I brought them in. Right now they're sleeping it off. All four of them. They wouldn't wake up if a stick of dynamite was to go off and the building was to fall down."

John Breckenridge eyed him narrowly. "Maybe you can tell me what I need to know. The bartender says Kramer lost his herd, gambling."

The sheriff picked up a pencil and held it with both hands. "What's that to you? Kin?"

John shook his head. "It so happens that I had a deal with him. We were running our herds north together."

"I see." The sheriff took a Bull Durham sack from his shirt pocket and expertly rolled a cigarette. "Now you're wondering if his herd will be going north this spring. Right?"

"Among other things." He pushed his broad-brimmed hat back on his head. "What's the new owner like?"

The sheriff shrugged. "He's the house gambler over at the Alamo. Man by the name of Rafferty."

"Was that game on the square?"

"As far as I know." He paused and lit the cigarette. "There's been loose talk about Sam runnin' a rigged table, but you hear that about every gambler."

John breathed deeply.

"It's a wonder your partner's still alive," the officer continued. "He got mighty careless the way he threw words around after he lost his herd.

If I hadn't been there he'd have been laid out at the funeral parlor next door."

John had another question. "How would this Rafferty be on the trail if the going got really rough?"

The sheriff leaned and crushed out the cigarette on the top of the potbellied stove, not answering immediately.

"Think he's man enough to hold up his end of things if he should decide to take the herd north?"

"Couldn't say. All I know for sure is that he quit his job at the saloon and said he was heading north."

Breckenridge had one hand on the doorknob when the officer called him back. "The trouble between Kramer and Sam Rafferty ain't over. Not by a long shot. The big guy who used to own the herd is boiling mad."

"I ain't surprised."

"To make matters worse he's got those cronies of his egging him on. They think the four of 'em can whip the world."

John smiled bleakly.

The sheriff continued. "If you decide to travel with Rafferty, it won't just be the faro dealer he'll be out to get even with."

"Sounds reasonable."

The officer reshuffled the papers on his desk. "I'm keeping the four of 'em in jail for a week or so. That'll give you and Rafferty time to get that herd out of here."

"You don't have to do that on my account."

The officer's gaze was as cold and bleak as John's own. "I just don't want any more killing in my county than I have to have."

31

The sheriff hadn't finished yet. "A week or ten days ain't going to do more than slow Kramer down. He'll catch you."

"I know."

"Keep your eyes open, cowboy."

John went back to his horse and rode to the hotel where Rafferty had a room.

The Queen Ann Hotel, in spite of its imposing name and false front, was like any other hotel in that part of Texas. The front door opened into the lobby. A number of rickety, aging chairs were scattered about the long room. Reflectored kerosene lamps were spaced at regular intervals along the walls with an extra lamp suspended from the ceiling above the desk where the night clerk lounged. It was getting late and the lobby was empty save for the slender, well-dressed individual who evidently was waiting for the clerk to figure his bill.

John eyed the one who was checking out. He had never seen the faro dealer before but recognized him immediately. He had the stamp of his profession about him. He wore the same dapper clothes John had seen cardsharps wearing in half a hundred saloons throughout the West. His hands were slender, clean, and well-manicured, and his hair was carefully slicked down. And he had that sallow, sickly complexion that came from spending too much time indoors. Sam Rafferty was smaller than most men. And he appeared to be strangely out of place in the West, a dapper little man with shifty eyes and a defensive manner.

Finally the clerk finished figuring the bill and Rafferty paid him.

Breckenridge followed him out of the building to the boardwalk. "Rafferty?"

The gambler whirled, palming a derringer that had been in his sleeve. "Don't try it, mister!"

"Put that thing away," he said. "I only want to talk to you."

His statement did nothing to allay Rafferty's concern. "I won those cattle fair and square!"

"That's what everybody tells me."

"I didn't want him to risk his herd. But he wouldn't hear to quitting. Kept saying I had to let him keep on so he had a chance of winning back what he'd lost."

"I can imagine how hard you talked to get him to quit," John murmured.

The gambler's expression changed. "I ain't been running that faro table for my health," he countered.

John could feel the tension in the other man. "That isn't why I came to see you. I've got three hundred fifty head running with Kramer's. We were fixing to go north together."

Rafferty's eyes slitted and his voice raised slightly. "I s'pose you've got papers to prove they're yours? Those three hundred fifty head you're claiming."

"I've got papers," John repeated. "Better than that, they're branded and earmarked. The whole three hundred fifty head."

Rafferty swore. "That lyin' Johnny Reb! He didn't tell me anything about you owning any of those longhorns. He claimed they was all his."

"I came to see you to find out if the deal I had with Kramer is still on."

The gambler put the small handgun away and for the first time since John Breckenridge had accosted him he relaxed. "You've made the trip north before?"

"I've made it before."

Rafferty breathed deeply. "Then you sure ain't going to have any trouble with me about going along. My pa used to have a cow on the farm back in Illinois when I was a kid. I had to milk her, but that's all I know about cows. I'm going to need you or someone like you to help out—at least till I get the hang of things."

"Then we've got a deal?"

The gambler nodded. "We've got a deal." He paused briefly. "What do we do now?"

"First off, we'll need more drovers. Counting Kramer we're short four."

"That's what I've been doing the last hour. Finding more hands. I've got five men waiting over at the saloon. I figured I needed an extra in case somebody feels like they don't want to ride for me."

"They'll stay. But we can use an extra hand. Specially for getting those strays rounded up."

Breckenridge agreed to meet Rafferty at the saloon in ten minutes. On the way he stopped by the livery barn, gave the hostler a dollar, and had him get the horses Gilson and Murray were riding and take care of them until the riders were released from jail.

The tall, broad-shouldered cowhand repeated the order to pick up the horses immediately and rode to the saloon where Rafferty and the new drovers were waiting.

"The sheriff thinks we'd better be moving come daylight," Rafferty told him.

"Can't do that," John countered. "We had forty head spook and take off. We've got to round them up first."

The gambler frowned. "Maybe we ought to

34

leave them and start putting space between us and that ugly-tempered character. What's forty head?"

The muscles in John's jaw tightened and for an instant he saw something in Rafferty's eyes he didn't like. Was it fear? "Forty head is forty head. The chances are we're going to lose enough stock on the drive that we can't do anything about. I say go after those mavericks without worrying about Kramer."

Rafferty nodded his approval. "Suits me," he said hesitantly. "I just don't want trouble with Kramer if we can keep from it."

Breckenridge studied the gambler curiously, wondering how this unbalanced partnership would work out.

The following morning the first faint streaks of dawn were lighting the eastern sky when the trail camp began to stir. Cookie was the first to waken. He pulled on his pants and boots and, stumbling noisily around the wagon, built a fire and put the coffee on. As he fixed breakfast, he rattled pans and slammed doors in the improvised cupboard that had been built in the back of the chuck wagon. If any of the drovers were still asleep when Cookie got up he soon saw to it that they didn't sleep afterwards. One after another got out of his bedroll, dressed, and went over to the fire for a first cup of coffee.

When breakfast was over the men who relieved the night watch shook out their loops and roped the horses they would be riding that day. John left six men with the herd. The other six paired off and went into the arroyos and mesquite thickets searching for strays. Rafferty insisted on going with Breckenridge.

"If I'm going to be a cattle baron," he chuckled, "it's time I learned something about cows."

"You'd better wait until we get to Montana before you start spouting off about that baron stuff. There's a heap of rivers to cross and Indians to get past before we make it."

The gambler ran his hand over his day-old whiskers. It was probably the first time in all the years he had been on his own that he hadn't shaved and trimmed his neat little mustache. No one used to seeing him in the saloon would have recognized him without a second look. His well-fitting coat was grimy, and his shirt, minus the stiff celluloid collar he always wore, made him appear half dressed.

At the gaming table Rafferty was a "dandy." Men made fun of him behind his back, saying he ought to be waltzing with the ladies at a fancy party back East or sipping tea at one of those high-toned cafes. He didn't belong in a saloon or anywhere else west of the Mississippi. Now, the way he looked, he didn't belong anyplace. No respectable hostess would have admitted him into her home for any reason—and he certainly didn't belong on a cattle drive.

Breckenridge surveyed the gambler critically. "You ain't figuring on wearing that outfit all the time, are you?"

"It's all I've got."

"Then you'd better do something about getting some more duds. If you don't you'll scare every cow in Texas and probably get yourself cut to pieces on the cactus and mesquite and yucca."

"I ain't got time."

"You'd better take time. You try wearing that outfit herding cows and it'll be plumb tore off of you. You'll be naked as a jaybird before we get to Kansas."

Sam Rafferty allowed himself a bleak smile, then turned for a final visit into town.

Breckenridge and Ohrman, one of his own drovers, went into the low, rolling hills north of the draw where the main herd was grazing. The strayed longhorns hadn't drifted far. The men began to find them by twos and threes and headed them north to the main herd. Getting them back with the rest of the cattle was another thing. The stubborn beasts were ugly and ill-tempered and, like the men who were driving them, were determined not to be shoved around.

The bulls were the most difficult. They hid in the willows at the bottom of narrow arroyos or sought out the thickest mesquite. There they faced the riders balefully. Anger raged in their bloodshot eyes and their sharp horns were at the ready. For all of their size they were lightning fast with those long, wicked, swordlike horns, and many a rider had lost his mount or even his life to a sudden thrust that caught him unaware.

But Ohrman was a veteran of a dozen drives to the North. He knew what he was about. Together they rousted out half a dozen mavericks and forced them back to the herd. The rest of the men were experienced as well—even those Rafferty hired. As the day wore on the number of cattle still in the brakes diminished. Another two or three days and they would have most of the strays and would be ready to start north.

Rafferty rejoined the drovers as they gathered around the chuck wagon that night for supper. He was weary from the ride and uncomfortable in his stiff new pants and chaps and flannel

shirt. Everyone else was watching as he dismounted.

"What's the trouble, Sam?" Cookie asked his
weathered face inscrutable. "Got saddle sores?"

The gambler scowled and cursed under his
breath.

"You look right purty in them new duds. It's a
shame you'll have to get 'em dirty."

Rafferty loosened the cinch and jerked the
saddle from his mount. "Shut your trap!"

John Breckenridge got to his feet. He didn't
know Rafferty well so he had no idea how short
the fuse was that held his temper in check. But he
did know Cookie. He wasn't the kind to take anything from anybody—even the boss. One wrong
word and there would have been a fight—or a
shooting.

"Here, Sam," John said, picking up the coffee
pot and filling a cup with the scalding liquid. "Wash
the dust out of your gullet!"

For a brief moment Rafferty glared at the
cook, then turned and accepted the cup from
Breckenridge. Trouble was averted—at least for
the moment.

5

In two days they rounded up the strays. Most of the stubborn, hardheaded longhorns had been flushed from the mesquite brakes and arroyos and were forced, reluctantly, back to the main herd. More hard, weary days in the saddle might cut the loss, but from that point on the men would more than earn every maverick they brought in.

The drovers knew Kramer and they were apprehensive and anxious to be on their way.

"Ain't no use hunting for more of them pesky critters," an old drover said, biting a chew from the plug of tobacco he took from his shirt pocket. "We got about all of them we're going to get."

John stared over the dusty, noisy herd in the direction of the setting sun. The fiery ball was sinking behind a line of clouds on the horizon. Had someone else made the suggestion he would have taken it as a challenge to his authority. But Elihu Wiggins wasn't like the others. Nobody knew his age, but he was a tough old codger who had done just about everything and had been everywhere.

"I reckon you're right," Breckenridge said mildly.

"Course I'm right." He spit a thin stream of tobacco juice at the nearest spiny yucca, and the brown liquid ran down to the center of the plant.

"The boys are getting a mite restless. They'd like to get the herd on the move."

John's gray eyes narrowed and he lowered his voice. "Tell me something, Elihu," he said softly. "You know most of these men. You've ridden with them come storm and high water. Reckon they'll be with us when push comes to shove? Can we count on them?"

Elihu frowned, the lines creasing about his thin lips. "They ride for the brand." He spit again and wiped the tobacco juice from his mustache with the back of his hand. "They'll be there when you need 'em."

"What about Rafferty?"

Elihu's eyes narrowed. "Now he's something else. If I were you I'd watch him close."

"What do you mean by that?"

"What do you suppose I mean? Watch him!"

That night at supper John informed the men that they would be starting north with the coming dawn. Murmurs of approval swept over the camp and a burden seemed to lift.

"So," he concluded, "get your gear ready and keep a sharp eye out when you're on watch tonight. We don't want anything to keep us off the trail."

Excitement gripped the drovers and they broke into little knots after supper, talking in low tones. At last they were going to be on the move. The news wiped away the frustration and uneasiness that had been disturbing them since the stampede.

John went to the front of the chuck wagon, got into his gear, and removed a box of ammunition, which he transferred to his saddlebags. Rafferty saw what he was about and came over to him, his weasel-face sharper than usual.

"Expecting trouble?"

There was an oily sleekness about Rafferty, even in a flannel shirt and chaps—a furtive sharpness in his features and a surly twist to his mouth that caused John to shrink from him.

"I always expect trouble."

"The sheriff still had Kramer and his boys locked up when I was in town. I checked on that, special. They'll be there the rest of the week, like he promised," Rafferty went on. "He gave me his word."

"Have you taken a look at that jail? It ain't much shucks as a building. A ten-year-old kid could break out of it if he was a mind to."

The color faded from Rafferty's gaunt cheeks and fear briefly glazed his eyes. He licked his lips nervously. "Why ain't they done it before now if it's so all-fired easy?"

"I don't think it's going to happen for awhile."

The gambler rolled a cigarette and lit it, cupping his hands about the match to shield the feeble flame from the sudden blast of wind that was descending upon them from the west. "You've got a good reason?"

"Good enough. We're too close to town, for one thing. If they hit us here and anyone lives to tell it, a posse would be on their tails like stubborn on a mule."

Rafferty nodded.

"Besides," John went on, "if he's as smart as I think he is, he'll let us handle the herd for now. He'll want us to take the starch out of 'em and get 'em broke to the trail. He'll wait until our hands are plumb worn out and maybe sort of careless."

The gambler pulled hard on the cigarette and

tossed it carelessly away. John glared at him and moved forward, grinding the still-burning tobacco into the dirt with his heel.

"Keep that up," he growled, "and we won't have to worry about Kramer. You'll set fire to the prairie and scatter the herd to kingdom come."

"It's not that dry!"

"When it comes to cigarettes and prairie fires," he snapped, "it's always that dry! And don't you forget it!"

The gambler had been fidgeting under John's even stare. Now his bony cheeks were livid and his eyes blazed. "I ain't one of the drovers! I own this herd! You can't talk to me that way!"

Breckenridge moved closer, his finely hewn features wrinkling. "I've told you once!" he said, his voice ominously low. "I don't want to have to tell you again! As long as I'm trail boss on this drive I'm in charge. That means you'll see that them fags of yours are out before you throw them away or you won't smoke!"

"If I don't?"

"You'll have to answer to me!"

The gambler's fist clenched and his lean face distorted with rage. "I hired you! I can fire you!"

"Anytime you want to be shut of me," John said evenly, "just let me know! I'll take my men and my three hundred fifty head and you can go it alone!"

Disbelief marred the gambler's cold, emotionless features. "You wouldn't do that!"

"Try me!"

Briefly their eyes fought, then a smile lifted one corner of Rafferty's mouth and the ice in his voice melted slightly. "Know something, Breckenridge?" he asked. "I just believe you would."

"You can count on it!"

The other man's smile broadened. "There's no call for you to be so uptight. I don't hanker on setting the prairie afire any more than you do."

John nodded. "That's more like it."

"Only don't rile me the way you did just now. OK?"

John was stiff and unsmiling. "I've got a job to do. If I have to climb your frame, I'll do it. You'd just as well know that right now."

"You're a cantankerous cuss."

The young trail boss turned abruptly away. Rafferty was cold and unfriendly, with the unblinking eyes and swift, furtive movements of a rattlesnake. There was something about his pale, cadaverous features and the way his gaze drifted restlessly, even when he should have been relaxed, that indicated he trusted no one.

Breckenridge rode out to check the herd and the drovers who were keeping it together. The sun was resting on the far horizon, a low curve pinched out of round by the upward march of the thick black line of clouds that were climbing above the hazy reach of the prairie and the rugged, treeless hills in the distance. The weather had been good the past few days, but an uneasiness in his bones told him that was due to change. Unless he was badly mistaken there would be a chilling wind and cold, miserable rain before daylight.

"Keep a sharp lookout," he warned the night watch. "You hear?"

They thought he was talking about Kramer and nodded grimly. One or two loosed their rifles in the scabbards and studied the outer perimeter of the empty prairie as though they expected the former owner of the herd to come blasting into view at any moment.

Twice during the night John crawled out of his bedroll and surveyed the darkening sky as the clouds advanced, blotting out the stars. The cattle also sensed the approaching blow. As the storm neared they began to stir. Those that were bedded down got to their feet and began to snort and toss their heads. The clatter of horns rippled across the herd and an old muley cow stretched out her neck and lowed mournfully. Another took it up, then another and another. Soon the entire herd was awash with the sounds of unrest and impending trouble.

An hour later, when the first icy drops stung his cheeks, John pulled on his boots and got his slicker from the roll behind the saddle. It was on just such nights as this that difficulties could explode without warning. He had to make sure that every drover on watch was in his place and alert to whatever might happen.

The wind was harsh and raw and the rain stung the faces of the men as they circled the longhorns. John didn't have to roust out the others. As soon as the storm hit they were up, saddling their mounts and riding out to give the crew on duty a hand.

Toward morning the rain slacked off slightly, but the wind, still sharp as a skinning knife, drove the cold through the drovers' yellow slickers and flannel shirts, chilling them to the marrow of their bones. Yet no one complained. It was part of the job. Any cowhand knew that the cattle came first and the worse the weather the more important it was that they be out with the herd. It was dirty, tiring, disagreeable work and they loved every minute of it. Even nights like that.

The overcast stretched from horizon to horizon and the penetrating cold whispered that they would not see the end of the rain for a week. It would be tough on the men but the cattle would be easier to handle on the trail. Moving forward would take some of the salt and vinegar out of them.

John would have moved the cattle to grazing grounds for a couple of hours before starting the trek north, but he changed his mind. It was better to have the herd on the trail than try to hold them in one place. The old bulls would only take the storm a certain length of time before doing something about it. Bellowing their displeasure, they would turn tail to the storm and break past the hands to go their own way. The cows and young stuff would not be far behind and Breckenridge and his hands would be faced with the problem of gathering the herd and rounding up the strays. It was best to leave right away.

As soon as breakfast was over John led the fresh drovers back to the herd and began to crowd the cattle northward. At first they resisted, snorting and tossing their heads fretfully. The men worked hard, keeping the pressure on the stubborn animals but at the same time taking care not to frighten the volatile critters. Grudgingly the longhorns began to give way, pushing up the trail in an effort to put distance between themselves and the drovers. At last the muley cow that had previously assumed command made her way to the rim of the herd and struck out briskly. The others followed along behind.

John and the drovers were keeping the pressure on the herd. Later it would not be necessary. The long, hard trail and sparse grass would soon rob the cattle of the energy necessary to take off on their own, except in the most unusual of circumstances. Now, however, they had to be constantly on the move.

Breckenridge had chosen the hands for certain positions with the herd. He had Elihu Wiggins riding point on one side and another grizzled old-timer on the other. Back a third of the way, where the big herd bulged, the men riding swing were stationed. Farther back the flankers took charge, keeping the herd moving and forcing strays back into the herd. The youngest, least experienced hands rode drag.

John changed mounts that afternoon, choosing a broad-chested buckskin from the remuda. He took his position at the head of the procession with Cookie in the chuck wagon behind him. The wrangler had the remuda to the left of the wagon.

Toward afternoon he went back to Elihu.

"I'm going out and have a look around. Take charge, will you?"

"You won't see anything." Wiggins wiped the rain from his face with a grimy hand and shivered slightly, but there was no other indication that he was cold. "Kramer's not a fool. Why should he jump us here and have to drive these cantankerous critters all the way north when he can wait for us to do a good share of the job?"

"I'd feel a sight better if I knew for sure that he wasn't on our tail."

Elihu's smile lifted crookedly. "I reckon that's the best way of keepin' our scalps."

John touched the buckskin with his spurs and rode off into the rain and wind. He traveled less than half a mile when the storm swallowed the trail herd and he was alone. Hunching forward and ignoring the miserable wet and cold, he studied the ground for signs of hoofprints. It wasn't likely that he would find evidence of riders following them. Such a rain would soon wash away any trail that men might leave. Yet a storm could make them careless. They could leave sign in such weather they would never leave on a warm, sunny day. Breckenridge kept the buckskin plodding along while he stared intently at the ground. The cold drove through him but he ignored it. He had a job to do.

Spring was still young and the grass was as short and scattered as the hair on an old man's head. It was interspersed with small areas of rain-softened clay. That would make tracking easier, at least if the storm let up.

He had been riding half an hour when the rain eased. The wind fell off and the downpour became a drizzle. He paused and glanced up, hopeful that the clouds were beginning to move out, making way for warm, pleasant days and nights. But that was not to be. The clouds were once again unbroken. It was obvious the respite would be brief, but he took advantage of it.

He turned the buckskin forty-five degrees and angled back in the direction of the campsite they had left earlier that day. He hoped to intercept the trail of anyone who may have been watching them or following along behind. From time to time he directed his attention upward. The clouds were low and darker and more formidable and the wind was fretful and gusty. One moment it whispered in the scattered juniper like a gossiping woman; the next it blustered across

47

the prairies and up the steep slopes. When the heavens opened again, as they surely would, the drizzle would become a deluge and what was left of any tracks would be washed away. He had to work fast. While the storm dozed he urged his wiry mount forward, taking advantage of the brief respite to cover as much territory as possible.

John traveled parallel to the trail for several miles on the surefooted buckskin, crossed to the east of the herd, and came back on the other side without seeing more than the narrow spoor of a doe and two fawns. Just before dark he rode back into camp, unsaddled, and turned his mount into the remuda. Elihu and Rafferty were sitting cross-legged under the canvas fly, as close to the dying embers of the fire as possible.

"See anything?" Wiggins asked.

"Nope."

"Didn't figure you would." Elihu's watery eyes gleamed. "Course a body can't be too careful."

Breckenridge stared into the fire without speaking. It was true that he hadn't seen anything suspicious on his long ride. Still, a certain uneasiness gripped him—the feeling that something was about to happen. If Kramer was as clever as John thought he was, he might use the foul weather to make his move. True, waiting until they were farther north made sense, but it also made sense to attack when the enemy was least prepared to protect itself. The cattle were irritable and rambunctious, and the drovers had long since reached exhaustion. He pulled in a deep breath. Just thinking about the situation was enough to keep him awake nights.

An hour later, as darkness moved in, the rain

started once more. It came in the teeth of the sudden rising wind, torrents that drove through the canvas and couldn't run off fast enough, turning the prairie into a sea of mud.

Night finally crawled by and John got out of his bedroll and checked the drovers. All was quiet as usual. The men, miserable in the cold and wet, moved the herd out, allowing them to graze for a time before starting them up the trail. The longhorns wanted to turn their backs to the storm and drift with it. The drovers, their mounts in mud up to their fetlocks, had to push continually to keep the herd moving in the right direction.

That day passed and another and another, with the storm still nagging at man and beast alike. The prairie, as far as they traveled, was a quagmire. At times the downpour stopped, and once the clouds cracked momentarily above them to reveal a thin slice of pale blue sky. But for nine days and nights the rain held them in its viselike grip.

Every day John continued to make a wide circle around the slow-moving herd, searching for evidence that Kramer and his gang were moving closer. On some occasions he made the trip both morning and afternoon, but he saw nothing until the ninth day out when the wind changed and the rain gave evidence of easing. He left the herd shortly after noon, making the prairie portion of the circuit first. As he headed toward the hills he caught a flash of movement against the dark sky. Someone had been on the highest hill watching him!

6

For an instant John remained motionless. Moments before a rider had been on the crest of the hill, staring down at him. But he had been too intent on searching the ground to notice the rider until he whirled to leave.

That flash of movement ripped John's attention from the prairie and jerked him erect in time to catch a glimpse of the fast-moving figure on horseback silhouetted briefly against the slate-gray clouds. He was so far away and the maneuver was so quick he wasn't able to catch the color of the horse or the build of the rider. All he knew was that he was being watched and it had to be Kramer or one of his men. No one else would be so interested in stalking them in such weather!

He lifted the reins and nudged the powerful gelding with his spurs. The surefooted buckskin broke into a gallop, forded a narrow, newly-formed stream cascading down the steep slope, and jumped a clump of soap weed in his path on the way up.

John slipped his rifle from its holster, levered a shell into the chamber, and balanced the Winchester against the saddle horn. As he neared the crest of the hill he tightened the reins, pulling his mount back to a trot. Warily he scanned the area ahead, his pale gray eyes searching out every clump of mesquite and juniper large enough to hide a man and his horse. The rider could have deliberately allowed himself to be seen, knowing Breckenridge would come up to investigate. He would have the chance to shoot him in the back. A chill gripped John and he straightened quickly. At the same time he noted the bearing of his horse. The ears were motionless and the big animal's body was relaxed. He was sure, then, that the other rider had left the area.

At the top of the ridge he reined in and surveyed the scene around him, his senses keenly alert. It was no longer sprinkling and the wind had faded to a whisper. The rainwashed slope to the west still showed the savagery of the storm. Narrow trenches were cut by the force of the water, angling into a gully that formed a temporary stream down the steep hillside.

Satisfied that the stranger was gone, John dismounted and began to search the soft ground, his rifle still in his hand. Every now and then he looked around quickly. It was not difficult to find the tracks of the other horse. They were almost at the buckskin's feet, the well-formed hoof marks of a newly shod saddle mount.

Breckenridge studied them carefully. The man who was so anxious not to be seen was not a Sioux or Cheyenne. Indians didn't shoe their ponies. They didn't use saddles, either, and the figure he saw was in a saddle. The man who had left so hurriedly was white. And he was big, judging by the depth of the hooves in the clay.

He was also determined not to be caught—a disturbing element. The West was lonely country. A rider with nothing to hide would not have been in such a hurry. The longhorns were so close he would have known John was a scout and there was nothing to fear. He would likely have ridden down to talk and probably have gone back with John to spend the night. Eating from a chuck wagon was always better than what could be fixed on the trail and spinning yarns with the drovers was a welcome break from the tedium of being alone. But Kramer, or whoever was on that hill a few minutes before, had a reason for avoiding John.

Satisfied at last that he had seen Kramer or one of his henchmen, Breckenridge stepped back into the saddle and returned to the herd. He reached camp two hours after Elihu and Rafferty had stopped for the night. Cookie had a fire going and the big kettle was steaming. The hands already had eaten supper and most of the dishes were done, but the cook saw John approaching from the distance and kept the stew hot. Elihu saw him, too, and limped over to the remuda as the trail boss dismounted and loosened the cinch.

"Where's Rafferty?"

"Out on the line. He's on first watch."

"If you see him before I do, tell him I'm looking for him."

"You don't look all that happy, John," Elihu ventured, his wrinkled face somber. "See something out there you didn't like?"

"A rider's been setting up on that hill yonder, watching us."

Wiggins spit a thin stream of tobacco juice and wiped the stain from his whiskers with the back of his hand. "Kramer?"

John shrugged. "I didn't see him close enough to tell, but I'd guess it was him or one of his gang. Anyway, when he saw I was heading his direction he cut out like he'd been turpentined."

Painfully, Elihu drew his twisted spine as erect as possible. "I knew things were going too good to last."

John's eyes hardened. "If a scrap is what he wants, we'll see that he gets it!"

Elihu nodded, his wizened features taut as a Cheyenne medicine drum. "You're durn tootin'."

John got a plate of stew and sat down beside the weathered drover who was finishing a final cup of scalding coffee. In half an hour it would be dark, a situation to the liking of those hard men who must be lurking out there waiting for just such cover before attempting to steal the herd. Kramer might strike at any moment. John and his drovers had to be ready.

Elihu must have been thinking the same. "Want me to double the guard for tonight?"

John sipped the steaming liquid in his cup and set it down. "That's a good idea."

The old drover got to his feet.

"Tell the hands to keep a sharp eye all night," Breckenridge reminded him.

Wiggins stopped in stride and turned deliberately, disgust twisting his weathered face. "Son," he said, "I was fightin' rustlers before your ma had you weaned! I know what needs doing!"

Breckenridge let the old man alert the drovers. He was on a second cup of coffee when the extra hands rode out to take their places along the line. Elihu came and sat with him.

Cookie did the last of the dishes, put away the big kettle, and checked his supplies for breakfast. Come dawn he would have to be up, cooking again for fourteen ravenous hands.

John was restless. Loosing the leather thong

on the trigger of his six-gun, he sauntered over to the remuda and studied the horses, or what he could see of them in the growing darkness. All was quiet so far. But that didn't mean the outlaws weren't near.

He saddled a fresh mount and rode out to the gambler's station. Rafferty saw him coming and spurred over to him.

"Everything all right?"

"So far. But we're about to have company."

"Kramer?"

"I don't know anyone else with an interest in this herd."

Rafferty's cheeks paled in the semidarkness and John saw his lips tighten.

The gambler's eyes flashed. "I ain't turning them over to anybody."

"It'll mean a fight."

"Then we'll fight!"

"I just want to know where you'll be when the lead starts flying."

"Right alongside of you," he blustered, "with a gun in each hand."

John went back to camp, crawled into his bed-roll, and closed his eyes. He lay tensely on the ground, his rifle and his Colt Peacemaker under the worn blanket.

Twice during the night he saddled a horse and rode out to check on things. But all was quiet. Most of the cattle were bedded down.

Daylight came but the drovers did not let down their guard. The banter at breakfast was restrained and, frequently, a hard-bitten hand would put aside his breakfast and get to his feet to stare out across the flat expanse of prairie. The land, as far as one could see, was devoid of movement. The sun was still hidden by the unbroken sheen of cloud, and a haze hung in the arroyos and shrouded the distant hills. There were places everywhere that could hide a gang bent on keeping their presence a secret.

They moved the herd out slowly. The longhorns were easier to handle than they had been during the long, constant rain. Yet the drovers held them a bit closer and prodded them forward more consistently than before.

Rafferty, from his drag position, said little but John was aware that the gambler missed nothing. His beady eyes shifted constantly, taking in the hands, the wrangler moving the remuda, and the drovers ahead of him.

Wiggins moved closer and lowered his voice. "I'm going to tell you something for your own good. Kramer's like one of those Arizona sidewinders that scoots crookedlike over the sand. They come sliding up to you out of nowhere and the first thing is *bang!* They've nailed you! The only difference is that Kramer ain't going to warn you with no rattling. We'd best be ready or the buzzards'll be pickin' our bones."

"I ain't afraid of him!"

The drover frowned. "You ought to be. I'm plumb scared speechless when I think about going up against him. I don't hanker to tangle with him and that's the truth!"

Rafferty studied the old man critically. "Don't try to tell me that. You haven't been scared of anything in your whole life!"

Wiggins reached down and rested his stiff, arthritic fingers on the bone handle of his well-worn six-gun. "Anybody out here as ain't scared once in awhile don't keep his hair on his head where it belongs. I been feeling right uneasy about Kramer and that gang of his ever since we started north."

The clouds hung low over the rugged flatlands and pressed down against the lonely western hills. The wind, still biting cold, soughed mournfully over the short grass, and it looked as though it could rain again.

The drovers went about their duties without complaint. They hunched deeper into their woolen mackinaws and pushed the herd as rapidly as possible over the soaked ground, trying to get to the place where they would spend the night before the storm attacked again.

But the heavens remained dry and the day went well. Shortly after noon they reached a swollen river. The murky, churning brown water presented a formidable barrier for the half-wild longhorns spread out along the debris-choked stream.

John rode up and surveyed the situation.

The men and cattle were exhausted from the long trek in the rain and cold and wind. The safest thing would be to wait for the skies to clear and the river to go down, but the weather in Texas at that time of year was completely unpredictable. No one knew how long it might take for the stream to calm.

Rafferty and Wiggins came up behind John.

"Going to take them across now?" the gambler asked.

At that instant John made up his mind. The longhorns were tired and so were the drovers, but the Texas cattle had stamina few animals possessed. And they were in good shape. As for the men, they would sleep better if the river had been crossed.

"We'd best get it over with."

Elihu nodded his approval.

Cookie, who was responsible for the chuck wagon, took two hands and went upstream to a place where he remembered seeing some old cottonwood logs on a previous crossing.

They pulled the logs to the riverbank, lashed them to the wagon's running gear, and with a team of fresh horses pulled the chuck wagon into the water. The horses lunged wildly against the harness when Cookie put the whip to them. The lash cracked fearfully over their heads and they charged into the stream. Five minutes later both he and the wagon were safely on the other side and the horses were breathing heavily and trembling from exertion.

Only then did the drovers turn their attention to getting the cattle across. They roped the muley cow that had been leading the herd and pulled her toward the fast-moving current. She didn't like the idea of going into the water. She straddled her legs and bawled her protest to the sky. But the roper tightened the lariat on her horns and forced his mount into the wide stream. Walleyed with terror, she struggled savagely against the lariat, but it was useless. She could not resist the relentless force that pulled her into the river.

Once the shock of the icy water was gone and the lead cow was on her way—one tentative, hesitating step at a time—the herd moved timidly after her. The drovers on either side shouted and waved their hats. The first critters in the water were even more afraid of the strange noises behind them than the river.

The cowhands chose that moment to force the rest of the herd into the turbulent stream. The cattle were lunging towards the opposite bank. Those that hung back were prodded along by the press of the critters behind.

At least two dozen had other ideas. They broke away and bolted for the prairie, their great heads low and menacing. Riders spurred their frantic mounts out of the way to avoid being ripped by those ugly, swordlike horns. The instant the would-be mavericks were past the men rode recklessly after them into the water. Moments later the river was filled with leaping, plunging cattle, anxious to get out of that cold, frightening current as quickly as possible. A few tense, agonizing minutes later the last of the longhorns scrambled up the bank and stopped, straddlelegged, their sides heaving with exertion and terror.

John stared across the bony spines of the longhorns. They had made it without so much as the loss of a single cow. He expelled his breath slowly. Now, if the drovers had done as well, the crossing could be counted a success. Getting the herd over any stream was always dangerous, and flood stage made it even worse. It was more difficult for the men than their charges. The drovers took grave chances to keep the cattle moving smoothly. He had seen cowhands jostled off their mounts and swept away, not a dozen feet from the tips of his fingers while he watched helplessly. Others had been knocked free from their saddles and carried downstream by the raging torrent so swiftly no one could save them. He had seen men panic when they were thrown into a river because they couldn't swim. They struggled helplessly without grabbing a stirrup or their horse's tail and were swept out of reach.

On two occasions John had tried to save such men but he had been just as helpless, unable to do a thing. He had seen so much of accidents and death at such times that he always approached a river uneasily and was relieved when the crossing was made.

Rafferty spurred up to him, a smile twisting his bony features. "We made it!" he cried exultantly. "We got every last critter across! Didn't lose a one!"

John's lips tightened. "We crossed one river," he said. "But there are a heap more that we've got to face before we get where we're going."

"We've got a good bunch of hands. We'll make it!"

John was about to turn away when the gambler spoke again. "This calls for a little celebration."

"There'll be time enough for that when we get to Montana."

Rafferty ignored his remark. "I'm going to call the boys in and give them a couple of drinks."

Breckenridge frowned. "I told you there was to be no liquor on this drive."

The gambler's cheeks crimsoned. "Nobody can tell me when I can have a drink and that goes for my men." He swung out of the saddle, unfastened the saddlebag, and took out two bottles of whiskey, holding them by the neck. "Two bottles aren't going to do anybody any harm."

John whipped the Colt from its holster and fired twice, shattering the bottles and showering Rafferty with the fiery liquid.

The gambler's features paled and he stared at Breckenridge in disbelief. "You could've killed me!"

Two drovers moved closer curiously.

"When I said no liquor, I meant no liquor."

"One of these days you'll go too far!"

Calmly John kicked out the spent casings and reloaded. "Any time you're of a mind to make an issue of it, let me know."

The silence was taut between them.

Then a voice from the riverbank broke the silence. "Anybody seen Wiggins?"

At the name Breckenridge jerked erect. He had checked the drovers off mentally, one by one, but he had completely forgotten his old friend—the one man on the drive he was really close to.

Concern marred the faces around him.

"His buckskin's over here, still saddled!" someone else cried.

A chill swept over John and he spurred his mount to the river's edge where the hand who sounded the alarm was sitting his dun gelding.

"He was right beside me, John!" the drover cried, shaken by what he was afraid had happened. "I didn't think he was in any trouble so I went on. I didn't even think about him for a spell. When I did, he was gone."

Breckenridge turned his attention downstream, staring into the gray haze that grew thicker with each passing moment. It was certain that the old man didn't know how to swim. Most drovers were dry-landers who had never spent any time around water.

John took a youthful hand with him on the ride downstream. At first they saw nothing save a heavy cottonwood branch that must have fallen with the tip in the water.

"Think he'd float any farther than this?" the drover asked.

John's lips parted, but he stopped short, staring at a plaid shirt caught in the branches of a scrub willow that hung out into the floodwater.

"What's this?"

He swung to the ground and leaned forward. There was Elihu's lifeless body swaying in the strong current.

"Give me a hand!"

Together they dragged the dead man out of the water. As they rolled it over John saw the bullet hole in the back between the shoulder blades.

"What do you know?" the hand exclaimed. "He was shot!" He stared at Breckenridge. "Now, why would anybody want to do that?"

John stood, thinking back to the horse Elihu had been riding. There was only one other buckskin in the remuda and John rode that one himself. He pulled in a deep breath. The bullet hadn't been intended for his old friend! Whoever killed Elihu Wiggins thought he was killing him!

7

Breckenridge bent over the lifeless form of Elihu and examined the wound. He had been shot in the back. But the body had washed downstream so it was impossible for anyone to know where the gunman had fired from. He might be close by or two miles away by this time. The bullet could even have been fired from across the river. John touched the wrinkled, bewhiskered face, anger burning through his being. Why would anyone kill a likeable old man like Wiggins?

For a brief moment he did not move. The wind stirred restlessly in the cottonwoods overhead and a few drops of rain splattered on his hat and the bridge of his nose. Elihu had been killed. A chill shook him.

He turned and stared upriver at the grazing cattle and the dark forms of riders on horseback. Why did it have to be Elihu? Why had he been the one to use the buckskin that day? A sword twisted in John's belly.

"Get back to the herd on the double and tell Rafferty what happened. Have him double the guard and send a couple of men down here with spades. We've got to bury Elihu."

The drover vaulted lightly into the saddle,

raked the horse with the spurs, and raced for the herd. The lean hammerheaded animal stretched out along the ground.

The young drover galloped madly up to the chuck wagon, shouting the news that Wiggins had been killed. Rafferty and two sharpshooting hands grabbed spades, their rifles, and saddle horns, and sped back to John.

"What's going on down here?" the gambler cried.

John pointed to the body.

Fear stole the color from the gambler's cheeks, leaving them pale and sallow as a dead fish. A nervous tick worried the corner of his drooping left eye. "Was it Kramer?"

"The thought had crossed my mind," John retorted, his manner cold and deceptively calm.

"If he hits us when we're split up we won't have a chance!"

"We're going to bury Elihu first!"

"Then let's get with it!" He turned to the men who had accompanied him and shrilled, "Get that grave dug!"

Rafferty jerked his rifle from the boot and looked about frantically while the drovers worked. They were clumsy and inexperienced—men born to the saddle, not used to working with their hands. They spaded awkwardly through the tough sod and dug into the clay. John and his young companion were even more alert than the gambler. They, too, had their rifles across their saddles and were staring about them. Their attention stopped at every clump of brush, every dip and arroyo that might offer a hiding place for the gunman.

John said nothing, but he, too, was half expecting an attack by Kramer and his men.

In a few minutes the shallow grave was ready. They rolled the gray-haired drover's body into it and John, taking the shovel, filled it in himself. He wanted to pray over the grave when he finished but he couldn't think of anything to say that was appropriate.

Rafferty turned and started back at a hard gallop. They galloped briskly back to the chuck wagon. Breckenridge stopped long enough to see that everything was in order, then he turned his mount and began to circle the longhorns that were bedding down for the night.

"Where do you think you're going?" the gambler demanded uneasily.

John did not answer him. Rafferty disturbed him. He could handle himself with disgruntled losers across the table. But this was different. Here a dozen men might be shooting at him and he would lack the edge he always gave himself in a gambling fight. Breckenridge stopped and talked with the men on watch, making sure they realized how important it was that they keep alert. A few extra seconds' warning could make the difference.

When John finished checking the men on first watch he unsaddled and turned his mount to the wrangler. Then he went back to the chuck wagon where Cookie was putting away the dishes after the evening meal.

"Want somethin' to eat, boss?"

"Not tonight."

"You ought to have something. A man fights better on a full stomach."

John went over and stood by the fire.

"Give me whatever you've got left over. It doesn't matter."

"Pour yourself a cup of Arbuckle's Best and set. I'll get you something in a jiff."

For several minutes Breckenridge stared bleakly into the flames. After eating he got to his feet. "You got Wiggins's gear handy?"

Cookie's eyes slitted. "I reckon so."

"I want to look at it."

"He didn't have much," Cookie said.

John's lips tightened. "How would you know?"

Cookie stopped what he was doing and faced Breckenridge. "I went through it," he said. "Wiggins was the best friend I ever had! I wanted to see if he had any family I could write to."

"Maybe you overlooked something."

Cookie strode to the front of the chuck wagon, pulled out Elihu's gear and tossed it at John's feet. "See for yourself."

Breckenridge picked up the bedroll without comment and took it over to the fire. It was obvious that it had been thoroughly examined. For all the carelessness about the way he dressed, Wiggins was careful about his few possessions. Some of the men used to razz him about the time he took putting his stuff back together. Cookie had rummaged through it hurriedly, and even more hurriedly rolled it and tied it in a bundle.

John went through the old man's things item by item. He had three shirts, a pair of Levi's, and two pairs of work pants. Wrapped in the shirts was a Bible with an inscription on the fly:

TO MY HUSBAND, ELIHU.
CHRISTMAS 1851.
ESMERELDA WIGGINS.

Breckenridge thumbed through it thoughtfully. Although it was an old book it was apparent that it hadn't been read. Some of the pages were uncut and the binding was new and stiff. There had been a tragedy in the old man's past. Something serious enough to keep him away from the woman he obviously loved.

John checked the men on the line twice before crawling into his bedroll that night. He tried to sleep but he found it impossible. Once or twice he dozed off fitfully, but a sudden rush of wind through the trees or the lowing of a muley cow jarred him awake. He sat up quickly, his rifle in hand.

After every change of drovers he rode out to the herd, checking to see that the men were alert and that there was no sign of an impending attack. Then he came back and lay down again.

Morning was shrouded in fog. An opaque gray mist surrounded the cattle and hid the nearby river from view. Trees took on eerie shapes, twisted in form and half blanketed from view. The only sound was the restless bawling of the longhorns.

Cookie had been up for an hour, rattling pans and noisily building a fire. Cowhands got out of their bedrolls and saddled their mounts.

Breckenridge had finished breakfast and was lingering over a last cup of coffee when three riders appeared suddenly, coming up to the chuck wagon out of the gloom. They were clad in filthy Levis and ragged jackets. Their hats were stained with sweat and the grime of the trail and their whiskers were as grubby and nondescript as a winter-shedding mustang.

"Where's the boss man?" the spokesman demanded harshly.

John Breckenridge got slowly to his feet. "What's on your mind?" This was the showdown they had been waiting for, the introduction to the battle that was to follow.

"You've got some of our critters in that herd of yours and we don't like it much!"

"What's your brand?"

"Never mind that! We just came in to tell you that we're going in to take ours out."

John's hog-leg appeared suddenly in his right hand. "Make one move toward that herd and you're a dead man!"

The spokesman touched his mount with the spurs, and the horse stepped forward sprightly. "We'd like to settle this peaceable if we can."

"That's no problem. Just turn around and get out of here!"

For an instant the outlaws stared at him as though measuring his resolve.

"Just remember!" the spokesman grated softly. "We tried to be nice and not cause you any trouble. But you wouldn't hear to that." They turned suddenly, as though on signal, and disappeared in the early morning fog. For a moment the only sound was that of horses' hooves pounding on the hard sod.

"Think that's the end of them?" Rafferty asked hopefully.

"They'll be back."

Some of the drovers had seen the interchange. They dismounted, jerked their rifles from their holsters and took such cover as was available. Men were on the ground behind clumps of soap weed or crouched among the cottonwood and willow along the riverbank. Cookie retrieved his double-barreled ten-gauge from its place in the chuck wagon, checked to be certain it was loaded, and snapped off the safety.

Grimly the men guarding the herd waited. The only sounds were those made by the cattle and the wind playing in the trees. John rode out to the men on the line, warning them of what was to come. He wasn't back to the camp when the opening shot was fired. It came from somewhere in the opaque curtain of fog that seemed suddenly thicker and more impenetrable. A drover screamed in pain and bedlam exploded.

Half a dozen hard-riding outlaws charged out of the fog, their rifles roaring. Breckenridge raked the buckskin with his spurs and the big horse leaped into a hard run. He found a target in the form of an outlaw fifty yards away, zeroed in on him, and fired. His bullet caught the renegade in the hip. The rider lurched forward and had to grasp the saddle horn to keep from pitching to the ground.

Another hard-riding desperado had to swerve to keep from hitting John. The move was involuntary. He saw John looming out of the murky haze and jerked his horse to one side, narrowly avoiding a collision. As the horse and rider skinned past, Breckenridge struck out with the butt of his Winchester. The bandit grunted as the blow caught him in the stomach. He slumped forward and fell to the ground.

By this time the terrified cattle charged blindly away from the gunfight, sweeping across the bleak prairie and up the gentle slope. The drovers were hard-pressed to fight off the attack.

The outlaws pounded towards the chuck wagon file, firing wildly. Cookie waited calmly for the rustlers to come into range, the big barrel of his ten-gauge resting on the tailgate for support. He led the first bandit expertly and squeezed the trigger. A hole twice the size of a man's fist was blasted in the outlaw's belly.

Cookie touched off the other barrel. He missed his intended target but the roar of the shotgun alerted the would-be rustlers to the weapon he was using. They veered off as he reloaded.

The battle continued for another few minutes, but John sensed a change in the attack. The renegades had fallen back and the tempo of their firing began to slow.

"Come on!" Breckenridge shouted. "Mount up! Go after them!"

But the bandits were already beaten off. A few sporadic shots were touched off, and the fierce battle was over. They thundered away leaving two of their number dead and a third seriously injured.

For a moment or two all was silent, then Rafferty shouted exultantly. "We did it! We did it!"

Silence gripped the tense drovers.

"How'd everybody make out?" John asked. "Anybody hurt or killed?"

"Jim Peak got it!" a young hand exclaimed. "I think he 'bought the farm.'"

"He's dead, all right," somebody else said.

"How about the others?"

"I caught a slug in the hip," another hand said. "I don't think it's too bad but it hurts like blazes."

John Breckenridge checked the rest of the

men, then came back and cleaned up the thigh wound. Once that was accomplished he attended to the badly injured outlaw.

"Where was Kramer when the fight was goin' on?" he asked.

The bad man's lip curled in derision. "Who's Kramer?"

"You know well enough who Kramer is. What'd he do? Send the rest of you out to fight his battles?"

"I don't know nothin' about no Kramer!"

"He was out here. He had to be!"

The outlaw's lips tightened and he refused to say more. John finished cleaning out his wound and bandaging it.

8

With the rising sun the fog began to burn away, warming men and animals alike and quieting the prairie. There was little evidence that a fierce battle had been fought. All was as it had been, save for the overturned sod of three new graves. Soon weeds and grass would reclaim the mounds, and the secret of the battle would remain locked in the bosom of the prairie and the hearts of men.

John sent the drovers out to find the cattle and hold them together. There would be strays, but prompt action could keep them to a minimum.

Rafferty mounted his horse and stopped momentarily before Breckenridge. "I didn't think that would be so easy," he exclaimed. "We broke Kramer of suckin' eggs."

Breckenridge did not reply. He poured himself a cup of coffee. Cookie did the same.

"What're you fixing to do with Elihu's gear?" he asked.

John hesitated. "You can have his clothes if you're a mind to. I'll keep that Bible."

Cookie squinted narrowly at him.

John went out to the remuda, roped the Morgan gelding and saddled him. From the camp he could see the herd in the distance. They had run a mile and a half away, up a long slope to a flat, treeless plateau. The grass must have been good for they had stopped when they reached level ground and it didn't appear that they had scattered far.

He joined Rafferty on point. "Looks like we got a break for once."

The gambler frowned curiously.

"Those pesky longhorns didn't decide to run very far and I don't think we're going to be spending a week rounding up strays."

"I thought you were talking about getting Kramer out of our hair."

For a time John surveyed the distant horizon. "I wish." He hadn't planned on expressing his doubt to Rafferty right then that they had seen the last of Kramer and his men, but it slipped out.

The gambler swore darkly. "After he got the licking we gave him, you don't think he'll be back, do you?"

"I hope he don't, but I sure wouldn't bet on it."

The drovers spent the rest of the day counting cattle and checking the brakes and arroyos for strays. A few of the more ill-tempered had taken off, but the land was flat and lacked good places to keep out of sight. By dark John decided they had found most of the missing longhorns and had them back with the herd.

That night Breckenridge changed mounts and circled the area, searching for tracks that would indicate Kramer and his men were still around. He found the hoofprints that marked their retreat and followed them along the river at least two miles to the place where they forded. Across the stream they had built a small campfire, prepared something to eat, and moved on. For all intents and purposes they were heading out of the country. But that didn't sound like Kramer. He probably wanted Breckenridge and Rafferty to think he was giving up. But John wasn't ready to accept that. They had beaten off one attempt to steal back the cattle but Kramer would not stop with that. He would keep trying.

Early the next morning John and the drovers moved out again, still heading north across the vast, empty spaces of the prairie. Breckenridge rode around the herd in a huge circle at least once each day and some times twice. He found evidence of others in the area, both Indians and whites. There was one set of tracks that was particularly suspicious. Four men were traveling together five miles west of the herd. Though the cattle were moving slowly and the quartet following were on horseback, John saw their hoofprints five days in a row. Then they took off towards the northwest, hurriedly, according to the long strides evident in the sod.

As soon as he spotted the tracks he increased the guard and put out sentries a mile and a half away from the herd. Such men were to sound the alarm in case of another impending battle to give the main body of drovers an extra few minutes of warning.

Three days passed without incident. They stretched into a week—then two. Still there was no sign of the riders who seemed to be stalking the herd. John allowed the hands to relax slightly, though he still kept a sharp lookout himself.

He continued to scout the terrain around the camp. He came across several signs of Indian movement, but the Indians didn't appear to be hostile. The signs of travois poles being dragged along the trail were everywhere, which indicated they were traveling with their women and children, probably searching for game.

The herd was well into Kansas when two mountain men rode into camp with broad smiles and stories of their illustrious past. Lafe Saunders, the squat, broad-shouldered one with a belly that hung over his tattered buckskin pants and a voice that bellowed like a longhorn bull, monopolized the conversation. They had been on the trail for weeks without having opportunity to talk to anyone except each other. Now that they had an audience they were determined to make the most of it.

Mealtime came and, as was the custom in the West, they were invited to share the cook's handiwork.

"Don't mind if we do," Lafe bellowed. "That slop Amos's been a-servin' up lately ain't hardly fit for an Injun to eat."

His companion scowled. "You never let that stop ya from eatin' like a starvin' hound dog, and that's the truth!"

"A feller's got to keep up his strength."

"Your strength's all in your belly."

Lafe took the plate Cookie offered him and scooped a generous helping of beans and ham on it. Amos did the same. While they were eating John came over and squatted on his heels beside them.

"Where're you boys come from?"

Lafe snorted. "Where'd you expect? We're mountain men!"

Breckenridge nodded. The trapping had long since given out in the hills—at least on a scale that made furs profitable—but there were still a few men from the mountains who roamed aimlessly across the frontier, searching for a way of life that was no more.

"Have you seen anything we ought to know about? We travel mighty slow with these pesky longhorns."

"We seen lots of Indian sign," Lafe said loudly. "Scads of it!"

Amos turned on his companion. "He weren't a-talkin' to you!"

Lafe's feelings were hurt and he showed it. "You take so blamed long to say anything!"

"We seen Indian sign. Scads of it!"

"Hostiles?"

Amos's bewhiskered face crinkled. "What'd you say, Lafe?"

The corners of the smaller man's mouth drooped. "You're a-tellin' it. Go ahead! Get it all messed up."

"We never seed 'em," Amos continued thoughtfully. "But I've got me a hunch they was. Wouldn't you say so, Lafe?"

His companion was still pouting. He stared into his coffee cup and refused to speak.

"What'd you say?" Amos repeated, pleading with his companion for confirmation.

"You're allus wantin' to talk so much—go ahead. *Talk!*"

Amos got himself another cup of coffee. "I'd say they was hostiles!" he repeated. "Wouldn't you?"

"I'd say they was hostiles," Lafe continued. "Out to cause all the trouble they can."

"That's right!" Amos exclaimed, his features

lighting. "We seen that nester's cabin burned and all his livestock run off!"

Lafe turned on him irritably. "I was just fixing to tell about it."

"You never even thought about it," Amos muttered under his breath. "Not till I said it."

"How do you know what I thought of and what I didn't?"

Before the evening was over Breckenridge learned the details of the cabin burning—as much as the mountain men knew. The tragedy had happened a week or so before they stumbled upon the place. Someone else had been there first. There were no bodies in the burned-out building, but there were three fresh graves on a little knoll behind the house.

"You're sure it was Indians that did them in?" Rafferty asked.

"Ain't nobody else would burn a man out that way as I knows about," Amos said, "except maybe the ranchers where squatters has come in." He turned to his companion. "Ain't that right, Lafe?"

There was no reply from his companion.

"Ain't it?"

Lafe sighed his disgust. "Why don't you let me tell it?"

Exasperation edged Amos's voice. "Ain't we sure, Lafe?"

"I reckon so." He turned deliberately to Breckenridge. "If we was you, we'd figger on goin' the long way around—so's not to get into trouble."

"How far around?"

"I'd say like 'bout seventy-five or eighty miles east of here an' then north."

John made a quick calculation in his mind. "You're talking an extra two weeks."

"And that's a long time to be spending on the trail," Rafferty put in. "Extra time, I mean."

Lafe shrugged. "Ya asked us what we knowed and we told ya. You can do as ya please. It don't make no difference to us one way or t'other."

The mountain men left camp early the following morning, continuing their aimless wandering towards the southeast. John and Rafferty discussed the problem of Indians in the territory and the suggestion Lafe and Amos gave them to detour to the east to avoid Indian trouble.

Rafferty, still exuberant at their victory over the would-be rustlers, was all for continuing on their chosen course. Breckenridge knew they would be taking a chance going into a territory where there was Indian trouble, but two more weeks of travel would give Kramer just that much more time to hit them.

"I think we'd best stay on course, just like we planned."

They continued their journey northward for another ten days without incident. Still, John kept the drovers on the alert. The less experienced men, figuring the worst was over, chafed under the vigilance he insisted upon. Rafferty agreed with them. It was foolish to keep a double watch when the only evidence they had that hostiles were on the prowl came from a pair of addled old mountain men. But John would not relent.

They were in central Kansas when a small party of Sioux approached and wanted to talk with him. They stopped a hundred yards or so from the chuck wagon and the chief rode forward slowly, alone. The men off duty formed a line in front of the chuck wagon, their rifles at the ready.

Rafferty turned to John. "What is this?" he asked uneasily.

"He wants to talk."

"You aren't riding out there alone!"

"When they come like that, they're not going to fight. Not yet, anyway."

The gambler's lips quivered. "I hope you know what you're doing."

The chief, his eagle-feathered headdress glistening in the afternoon sun, rode his pony forward, one step at a time. There was dignity in the way he sat on his mount and in every move of his lithe brown body.

John noticed that there was no war paint on his face. That was an unmistakeable sign that he came in peace. John himself rode forward at the same slow, dignified pace.

The Indian leader raised his hand in greeting and John did the same.

"You drive your cattle over our lands!" he accused in the clipped, accented tones of one whose English was a second language.

"We didn't know it is your land."

"It all belongs to our tribe!" In a wide, sweeping gesture the Indian chief indicated that all they could see was the property of his people. "You pay to take your cattle across our land."

"We aren't fixing to stay. We're just going through. Three, maybe four days and we'll be out of your territory."

But the chief was not satisfied. "They eat our grass. You pay!" He hesitated. "Seventy-five cents for each cow!" He drew himself erect. "Cash money!"

"Too much." Breckenridge pretended to be thinking seriously about the demand.

"Seventy-five cents!" the Indian repeated firmly.

"Too much. I make you a present of two cows. Your pick."

The chief persisted in wanting to be paid in cash.

"How do we know the land is yours? You have paper?"

The Indian seemed not to understand. "Paper? What paper?"

"The paper that shows the land is yours."

He frowned. "The land is ours," he repeated doggedly. "It was our fathers' and our fathers' fathers'."

"You must have paper to prove it is yours. Then we will talk about pay!"

The chief continued his demand but the negotiations had changed. He was on the defensive now.

"No paper—no money!" Breckenridge refused to be moved from that position.

At last the Sioux leader pulled himself erect, eyes flashing. "We will see!" With that he whirled his pony and raced back to his braves.

John watched until they galloped away. Then he went back to where Rafferty and the men were waiting.

"Now what was that all about?" the gambler demanded uneasily.

John told him what had taken place.

"You didn't give in to the thieving rascals, did you?"

"Not so's you could notice. But we're going

to make them a present of two critters."

Rafferty swore. "Over my dead body! You've got to be out of your mind wanting to give those savages some of our herd! Do that and they'll be wanting all of them."

"We shamed the chief when we hit him with that bit about the paper. We backed him down in front of his braves. A gift of cattle will help him to save face as well as feed their families."

But Rafferty didn't agree. "You sure don't know Indians and that's a fact!" His voice raised. "Give them an inch and they'll think we're scared and they'll take a mile."

"They've got families to feed," John explained. "If we give them meat they'll be on their way and leave us alone."

"Maybe." The gambler was still unconvinced. "But I still don't like the idea of giving in to them. It plumb sticks in my craw."

"That's what we're going to do. There's no cause to have trouble with them if we can keep from it. It won't hurt us letting them have a couple of steers. And I've got me a hunch that'll keep us from bad trouble."

9

Breckenridge knew the Sioux and their ways. Shortly after the chief and his men rode off he had two drovers cut out two head of young stock and sent them to the Indian camp as a gift to the chief. When the men returned he called them to one side and asked what had happened.

"It was some sort of strange rite," the younger hand said. "I didn't know what was going on. Some kind of a dance or religious something or other. Anyway, they were playing drums and singing loud as anything. When they saw us coming a dozen or so braves circled us and took us to the chief and the elders. When we finally got him to understand that the steers were a gift he took them and ordered us to leave. He made it plain that we weren't welcome, so we cut out."

Rafferty was furious. "What'd I tell you? It doesn't do any good to treat them like they were civilized, go-to-meetin' Christians. They're bad all the way through. Treat them decent and they'll turn on you every time."

But Breckenridge was unconvinced. "I figure it's worth the risk."

"You'll find out how much it helps. We're still going to have a fight on our hands."

"Maybe. Maybe not." Breckenridge stood in

the stirrups and, shading his eyes with a bronzed hand, studied the low, rolling, treeless hills around them. Three Indians, astride their mounts, were watching from a distance.

He knew why. Always cautious, they wanted to know what the white men were going to do. Did the gift come from the heart as a sign of peace and good will, or was it a move of treachery?

John was not so naive as to believe the Indians who had accosted them were actually on their own territorial grounds. This was Cheyenne country and the chief and his men were Sioux. They had no right to charge anyone for the privilege of crossing that section of northern Kansas.

They were probably wondering if they had actually deceived the white men. Breckenridge grinned. If the Indians thought they had taken advantage of him and his companions, it didn't bother him.

Rafferty, however, had other ideas. He was still angry because of John's decision, seeing it as a sign of weakness that would come back to haunt them.

"Every Indian in the whole country is going to get the idea they can feed off us."

"There's no use arguing. It's done." John's features darkened, but he did not continue. They were going to have problems enough before the drive was over.

He made a wide scouting circle that afternoon, keeping a sharp watch for Indian sign. From the high ridge where he had seen braves two hours before, he reined in.

It was obvious that no one expected difficulty on such a day. The June sun warmed the ground and coaxed the early summer flowers into bloom.

A faint breeze whispered over the greening slope, teasing the newly forming milkweed pods and toying with the broad green leaves of the Spanish sword.

It was still early enough in the season that the harsh heat of summer was not in evidence. A few billowing white clouds marked off a corridor for the sun, and the moisture of spring brought a splendor to the land—a splendor Breckenridge never ceased to marvel at.

For a time he remained motionless, studying the landscape. In the area immediately below he could hear the barking of dogs and the excited voices of kids at play. He had expected the Indians to move on, but they were still close by.

The following morning the drovers moved the herd a short distance to better grass and allowed the cattle to graze while the men had breakfast and broke camp. By noon they were in a stretch of low hills dotted with sage and cacti and a few grotesque outcroppings of limestone.

It was much drier there and Breckenridge sent scouts ahead to locate the nearest water. What they found would decide how fast the longhorns would have to be moved. Furthermore, Kramer and his gang were always on his mind.

John left the herd shortly after sunup and rode west down a deep swale. From a distance it looked like swampland, but the valley was dry and hard as flint. He angled along the arroyo for half a mile, studying the path worn in the hard-packed soil. The trail ran parallel to the route the cattle were traveling and was quite well hidden, making it ideal for Kramer's purpose. John saw no telltale hoofprints nor the sign of recent fires, but constant uneasiness nagged at him. He had a strange

feeling that there was something he was missing—something that he ought to see if they were
to be forewarned about the former owner and his
plans. He paused momentarily near a clump of
twisted willows and studied the ground around
him.

At first he noticed nothing that would indicate
anyone else had been close. After a time, however, he saw a broken sprig of sage and below it the
indentation of a shod hoof neatly cutting the sod.
He made sure he wasn't being seen and dismounted to bend over the hoofprint.

Someone had been traveling the obscure
trail—and not long ago. He knelt warily and studied the marks in the ground. Whoever it was had
been anxious not to be seen. Only the slightest
indication of hoofprints was evident.

Thoughtfully he rode on, his gaze moving
constantly. He missed nothing. His hand was never far from the butt of his rifle.

John traveled several miles along the narrow
trail. It was so obscure in places he lost sight of it
completely and had to ride on a hundred yards or
more before locating it again.

He came to a place where the strangers had
stopped for the night beside a stream. The sand
leading down to the water's edge was chewed and
cut by the hooves of twenty or more horses.

He could not understand why Kramer—if he
was the leader of the outlaw band—had been so
careless at the stream. The only thing he could
figure was that they had gone for so long without
being detected that he began to get indiscreet. Or
perhaps he felt he had so many hardened gun-
fighters it didn't make any difference whether or

not Breckenridge and Rafferty knew he was back there.

Back at the herd, a drover coming in for a meal called to Rafferty and showed him a fresh steer hide.

"How long's it been?" the gambler demanded, his anger rising.

"It could've been last night or even this morning. But whenever it was they were mighty bold. Didn't even take it over the hill to do the butchering."

"Looks like the work of those pesky Indians to me."

"It's got to be them."

"We have to teach them a lesson!" Rafferty exploded. "Breckenridge insisted on giving them a gift of good white man's beef! But I knew it wouldn't work."

The gambler studied the distant hills, his eyes slitted against the brilliance of the sun. "Get the drovers. All we can spare." He spoke decisively. "Have them meet at the chuck wagon."

The youthful hand's eyes lighted expectantly. He was eager to test himself in a real fight. "Are we going after them?"

"You can bet your bottom dollar we're going after them. And this time we aren't letting Breckenridge talk us out of it!"

Rafferty rode back to the chuck wagon and dismounted. "Are those special boxes in the wagon?"

"Right under the driver's seat where you put them."

"I want to get them out, but while I'm at it

you had better make up a fresh batch of coffee," he ordered briskly. "The men'll be comin' in any minute."

The cook's bloodshot eyes drooped thoughtfully. "Did John find Kramer out there?"

"Breckenridge doesn't have anything to do with this! I'm taking over the herd from now on!"

"He knows this country, Rafferty," the cook reminded him. "It might be smart to leave him alone."

Anger flamed in the gambler's eyes. "When I want your advice I'll ask for it!"

Cookie shrugged his indifference. "Go ahead. Run things your own self. It ain't water in my beer."

By the time John rode back into camp the drovers were gathered in a ragged semicircle near the chuck wagon. The trail boss read the dark features of the drovers and caught the angry flush in Rafferty's cheeks.

"What's going on here?"

"It's them blasted savages!" the gambler exploded. "They butchered a steer in broad daylight."

"You're sure it was Indians?" he asked.

Rafferty glared at him. "If I weren't we wouldn't be going after them."

John dismounted and approached the cattle owner. "We'd better talk before we take on the Sioux."

"Before we talk there's something I've got to show you."

The two of them walked to the front of the chuck wagon together. Breckenridge stared down at the two long, rectangular crates.

"Are those what I think they are?"

"I don't know what you think they are." Rafferty's eyes sparked fire. "We gamblers like to call it a little leverage. A bit of special insurance."

"What kind are they?"

"Brand new .76 Winchesters with a couple of Sharps buffalo guns in case we've got somebody we need to put the fear into."

"Wished you'd have told me that. I'd have slept a sight easier on the trail."

While they were talking the gambler had one of the hands open the crates and begin to carefully wipe the grease from the rifles. John picked up one of the Winchesters and noted the button tubular magazines. It was a fine, no-nonsense weapon, superbly made.

"That's why I decided we've got to show those Sioux a couple of things. We can find out what these guns can do in a fight."

"There'll be time enough to see what they can do against buffalo or antelope without using them on men."

"I'd like to know what they'll do when the other guy's shooting back."

A great weariness took over John. "I still say, 'no.'"

"I'm going to make them pay for what they've done."

"That's a rough row you're trying to hoe. Those Sioux don't go down easy."

"We'll give them a taste of their own medicine."

Rafferty spit contemptuously into the dirt. "I suppose you're fixing to tell us that Kramer and his gang are about ready to hit us."

"That ain't all. He's got plenty of help. Maybe twenty riders."

The gambler saw the uncertainty in the drovers' eyes, the sudden questioning of his judgment and authority. "You saw what we've got to fight him with. Let him come. We can take care of him."

Breckenridge managed a humorless smile. Rafferty caught the look and his temper flared. "What're you trying to do? Make fun of me?"

"Nope."

Rafferty pulled out his watch deliberately and squinted at it. "We'd best be on our way." He turned back to Breckenridge. "You comin', John?"

"Not this time."

Rage twisted the gambler's sharp features. "Are you refusing to follow orders?"

John's voice was even and quiet, yet there was a forcefulness in his voice that was unmistakable. "You could call it that."

"Then get your gear packed and be on your way! We don't need your kind around here."

One of the drovers, an older man who had ridden the trail many times, turned to Breckenridge. "You taking off, John?"

"I reckon so."

The grizzled cowhand wiped his broad hand across his face. "Then I'm leaving, too."

"So'm I," another said.

"And me. If push comes to shove, I ain't looking to run out on no fight. But I ain't hankerin' to go out of my way for trouble, neither." He turned to the gambler. "Give me my pay, Rafferty. I'm stringin' with Breckenridge."

The gambler's hawklike features contorted angrily. "What are you trying to do?" he demanded. "Ruin me?"

"Nothing. Nothing at all." John turned to the drovers who had indicated they wanted to go with him. By this time there were five. "You'd best stay with Rafferty."

"You're not fooling me! I know what you're up to. You're just like Kramer. You won't be satisfied until you get my herd."

John's eyes iced. "Careful, Sam!"

Rafferty jerked the derringer from his sleeve and started to squeeze the trigger, but he was too late. John read the sudden move, whipped out his own weapon, and fired before the gambler could pull the trigger. A spot of blood darkened Rafferty's shirt. His fingers relaxed, allowing the gun to slip to the ground. With his left hand he clutched the wound.

"You shot me!" he cried.

"Don't ever try to pull a gun on me again," John grated. "The next time I might not be as careful."

"I'll kill you for this, Breckenridge!" Rafferty gritted. "I'm a-warnin' you! I'll kill you! You can't talk to me that-a-way and get by with it!"

10

Breckenridge ignored the fury in Rafferty's voice. "Want to take care of that arm?" he asked Cookie quietly.

The cook's weathered features wrinkled distastefully. "I reckon so, but I ain't staying on with him."

For the first time helplessness gleamed in the gambler's eyes. "We had an agreement!"

He stared desperately from one drover to the next. The younger, more impetuous hands who were spoiling for a fight were standing by the gambler. The experienced men—those who would be cool and knowledgeable under fire—had aligned themselves with Breckenridge. Rafferty realized the difficult position he was in.

"You can't do this to me!"

"Nobody's doing anything to you, Sam," the cook broke in. "There isn't any one of us who ever left a herd before the drive was done. But this is different!"

The gambler read the concern in the eyes of the older men. Slowly his expression softened. "I–I reckon I got out of line some," he said, trying to smile. "You'll stay, won't you, John?"

Breckenridge hesitated. Lining up with the gambler again might be the source of more trouble. "I'd have to think on that."

"I didn't mean anything, especially against you."

"You pulled that gun on me. If you'd had your way the boys would be digging a hole for me about now."

A wry smile twisted the gambler's lips. "You taught me a lesson I won't forget. I've never seen anyone shuck an iron like you did."

"It helps when it comes to staying alive."

"Let's put all that behind us." Rafferty stepped forward, holding out his left hand in a gesture of friendship. "How about it? You'll stay, won't you?"

"What about traipsing off after the Sioux?"

"If you say 'go after them,' we go. You say 'don't' and we don't."

"No more arguments?"

"No more arguments. About anything."

Breckenridge breathed deeply. "OK," he answered, a certain reluctance in his voice.

Cookie cleaned and dressed the wound in Rafferty's upper arm. Fortunately the slug had gone through the flesh without hitting a bone.

John tore a piece from the tail of his clean white shirt and gave it to Cookie who soaked the rag in the whiskey and swabbed out the wound. Once he had it as clean as possible, he tied it around Rafferty's arm.

"Hurt much?" he asked.

"What d'you expect?" The gambler's head raised and fire flamed in his bloodshot eyes. Breckenridge saw then that the trouble between them was not over. It had been pushed aside because Rafferty knew he had to have help. The hatred was still there.

91

That night at supper John quieted the men and told them what he had found on the trail that afternoon.

The drovers stared at one another in silence. Most were not inexperienced when it came to fighting. They were grim, hard-bitten men who used their guns as a part of their job. They had been expecting it.

Rafferty sat alone, some distance from the others, staring sullenly into the fire. "We've got a dozen good men with the best rifles in the territory. We'll hold our own."

There was no sign of either Kramer's gang or the Indians that night. The following morning they began the long trek north once more. As soon as the longhorns were on their way, John scouted the prairies and hills along the trail. He made his way up the still barren slopes to the west and down into the arroyos and brakes. He searched every path, every game trail, for a sign of horses' hooves or the remnants of a camp fire.

He found no evidence that Kramer and his men were anywhere near. The day before he had seen sign of at least two dozen horses and twenty men. Now there were none. That didn't mean they weren't there. They just weren't leaving sign. That disturbed him even more.

John had been seeing Indian sign earlier. Now that, too, disappeared. The marks of travois poles had been evident in the clay trails and the scattered remnants of waste along their path indicated the movement of sizeable groups of people. He came across frequent campsites and the ashes of a number of cooking fires.

A strange uneasiness came over him. After weeks on the trail with only one half-hearted attack, the time for the major assault was surely close.

John checked the herd guards and made sure that everybody doubled the supply of cartridges they were carrying. Only Cookie saw both the calmness in his manner and the cold flames in his gray eyes. He poured a cup of coffee and came over to where Breckenridge was sitting, staring into the dying embers of the fire.

"Expecting something tonight?" the cook asked him quietly.

"Maybe. Maybe not." He breathed deeply.

"There's going to be trouble. I feel it in my bones!" Cookie finished his coffee in silence, poured the grounds into the fire, and filled the cup again. John did the same.

Shortly after dark Breckenridge circled the herd once more, checking each drover on guard. Rafferty joined him at the remuda.

"Looks quiet tonight," the gambler said.

Breckenridge unsaddled the buckskin and turned him in with the other saddle horses. Then he roped the dun gelding he also used, saddled and bridled the fresh mount, and tied him close to his bedroll where he could grab him in an instant.

He crawled into his bedroll, his Winchester under the blanket, and closed his eyes. The gambler was right about one thing. It was peaceful and quiet. It hardly seemed possible that there could be trouble on such an evening.

He dozed a time or two early in the evening before getting up and checking on the herd. Shortly after midnight he stirred up the fire, put the coffee on to boil, and sat for awhile, studying the night. Half an hour later he went back to his bedroll but not to sleep. He was up when the guards changed and again shortly before dawn.

A few scattered clouds drifted across the starred sky, hiding the moon, and a gentle breeze whispered over the prairie and through the willows that lined the nearby creek. It was colder than Breckenridge had thought it would be and he got his mackinaw from his gear in the wagon.

Cookie heard him rummaging through his things and stirred restlessly.

"It's just me. Go back to sleep."

"Everything all right?"

There was no time to answer. A shot rang out and another and another in close succession. The fusillade was followed by the sudden pounding of horse's hooves.

Breckenridge threw himself to the ground, levered a shell into the barrel of his Winchester, and fired three rounds as rapidly as possible. By this time the drovers were all awake, firing from whatever vantage point they could find.

With the first wild shooting the longhorns bolted. They charged across the grasslands, their hooves beating out thunder over the hard ground.

The hands under John's direction returned fire, shot for shot. Two rustlers went down, dead or dying. A third had his horse shot out from under him and was only able to get away by swinging up on the back of another's mount.

Breckenridge didn't know what Kramer and his men expected. But after the first barrage of rifle fire, they rode off and all was quiet once more. In the stillness that followed, Rafferty crawled over to where John was waiting.

"What do you expect now?" he asked.

"They had a little go at us. Guess they wanted to find out what we're made of. But they haven't even started. They'll be back and we'll have a real fight!"

By this time the first gray hint of dawn was softening the fierce blackness of the night. It lightened the eastern horizon and streaked upward across the sky. Whatever they did to get ready had to be done immediately, before Kramer and his gang cut loose once more.

Breckenridge called to Cookie and the wizened cook left the chuck wagon and dashed to his side.

"Take four or five men down in the willows along the creek," he ordered. "Get them settled in behind anything they can get behind. Have them hold their fire until Kramer's men get close enough to make it count."

Cookie left on the run, dashing through the semi-darkness. He picked several good, experienced hands and led them into the brush. John found the others and spaced them as best he could in the time remaining. Three men lay on their stomachs beneath the wagon. Others were scattered behind clumps of limestone outcroppings and in shallow depressions and fingerling ravines. Breckenridge mounted his horse and waited.

The second phase of the attack was not long in coming. With the spread of light along the eastern skyline the gray shapes of men and horses were more clearly visible. That was what the outlaws had been waiting for. They rode wildly, guns barking. A youthful drover, the one who had been so eager to attack the Sioux, was the first to fall. He had been carefully esconced in a narrow arroyo, but in the confusion he jumped and ran. He hadn't moved more than thirty feet when a bullet caught him. He stopped suddenly, drew erect for an instant, and collapsed.

Wild anger surged through John's veins. The drover was just a kid. Now he was dead! And for what? A man's stupidity and greed!

He spurred the powerful dun and the horse surged forward. His rifle came up and he fired at a rider racing toward him. The big, broad-shouldered outlaw pitched from the saddle and sprawled headlong in the grass. His mount raced off, stirrups flapping.

Breckenridge caught a glimpse of Rafferty crouched behind a clump of cottonwoods near the creek, his weapon belching flame. John had to give him credit. He was still in there firing.

John dashed furiously from one place to another, sending the men into different areas and leading them in the attack. He felt a bullet sear his side just below the rib cage and another screamed across his mount's back, slashing a reddening furrow in the mouse-gray hair.

And still the outlaws kept coming like men possessed. They, too, were suffering casualties—perhaps as many or more than the defenders. But there seemed to be no end of them. Kramer had taken no chances this time. He saw that he was prepared.

The battle continued without letup, ranging from the chuck wagon as far as the creek. The death toll was heavy. Four drovers were sprawled on the prairie near the wagon and John had heard no fighting from the creek in several minutes. He turned towards the creek, bending low over his horse's head and urging the big, hard-running mount faster and faster.

A hundred yards beyond the chuck wagon Breckenridge felt his horse stumble and almost go down. The dun righted himself and plunged on. But again the valiant animal went down on one knee. John slammed forward into the hard sod.

11

The sun stole silently skyward, washing the battlefield in the harsh white light of early summer. The wind was subdued that morning, leaving the leaves motionless on the scrawny, drought-twisted trees that lined the creek. Great billowing clouds strolled leisurely across the azure sky, bringing hope that the rains would not be far behind.

Vultures wheeled majestically above, riding the airwaves on almost-motionless wings. A coyote padded silently up from the creek, picking his way through the carnage the brief battle had left. The stench of death was upon the land. John Breckenridge lay unmoving on the hard-packed clay. The coyote nosed the back of his head and he stirred slightly. The mangy animal slunk furtively away, disturbed at finding the man still alive.

As the hours passed the cool of morning gave way to the heat of mid-day. The searing rays of summer were not yet upon the prairie, but the threat was poorly hidden. The higher the sun climbed, the more the heat intensified. The wind stirred slightly, nipping through the trees and blossoming soap weed, amid the splendorous array of spring prairie flowers.

Breckenridge groaned and lifted his head

slightly. He wanted to slake the terrible, burning thirst that had taken hold of him, but he could not. The effort to raise himself robbed his powerful frame of strength and he collapsed again on the ground. Everything went black.

He didn't know how long he lay there, drifting in and out of consciousness. The sun went down, and with the coming of night the cold wrapped itself about him. A terrible chill seized him. His very being quivered and he could not stop shaking until he was so exhausted there was no strength left in his body.

His back and side were caked with blood that had soaked his shirt and trousers and stained his chaps. The bleeding had slowed but had not yet stopped. Fresh red blood oozed from the wound between his ribs and hip bone.

He was dimly aware of the fact that it was still dark and very cold. The frigid air helped shake off the blurring of his mind, at least for the moment. He raised himself on one elbow and looked around. He didn't know what happened after he took that bullet in the back, nor how many were dead and scattered over the battleground. The drovers had fought valiantly. No one could have expected more of them, but they were no match for Kramer's hired guns.

Slowly the strength faded from his big frame. He collapsed once more, his breath coming in short, shallow gasps. For a time he lay as one dead or dying.

Morning came, and high noon, and the pleasant warmth of the latter half of the day. The clouds that had been gathering steadily were thick and black on the western horizon. The sun was about to slip behind the heavy screen, and the warmth of the afternoon began to fade.

John stirred restlessly, only half aware of where he was or what was going on about him. The fever that had come a few hours before was raging. His lips were swollen and dry and his throat choked. Pain hit him in great sledgehammer blows.

Water! He had to get water! His tortured mind tried to tell him that there was a huge, shallow lake not far away. A lake filled with cool, clean water. All he had to do was find it and all of his troubles would be over.

He raised his head again, shaking it to clear away the fuzziness. There was water close by. He was sure of that. There had been enough to water the cattle. Twenty-five hundred head would have required a stream or a sizeable pond.

Perhaps the lake that was stamped so indelibly on his mind was a reality. If only he could think! He had to find water and soon. He tightened his fist and slammed it against the hard ground! Why couldn't he think?

Grimly he put down his hands and, clenching his teeth at the aching torment that wracked his body, he forced himself to raise on one knee. He saw Rafferty's mount lying a few feet to one side and behind him. Already the heat had begun to swell the horse's belly. Behind the dead horse lay the body of one of the drovers, sprawled grotesquely in the grass.

He tore his gaze from the cowhand's lifeless frame and looked beyond at the growth of willows that marked the narrow stream. He remembered now! There had been a stream nearby, clear and cold and wide. Hope surged through him. If only he could make it to the creek and drink his fill of water! He tried to stand but stumbled forward and went down.

But he was not beaten. If he couldn't get to his feet he would crawl! He was not going to give in without a fight. He managed to raise his pain-tortured body off the rough ground and crawl forward, inches at a time.

The movement opened the wound and he felt the warm, wet blood flowing again. *The bleeding must be serious if I can't get it stopped.* He forced the thought from his mind and directed his effort toward crawling to the trees and the stream beyond. He didn't know how long it took to make his way to the stream. Several times his mind blacked out, but as soon as he regained consciousness he continued to struggle on, inch by painful inch.

At last he reached the stream and pulled himself close enough to splash the water on his burning face. He wanted to drink deeply, filling his stomach with the life-giving liquid. Yet he had to be careful, drinking a little at a time.

Once he had water a peace he hadn't known before swept over him. For a time he slept. Night settled in and with it a chill that awakened him. It set his teeth to chattering and his body trembling. The wind came up with a rush and it started to rain. He was soon shaking violently. With effort he pulled himself back from the creek and found a measure of shelter under the willows. He lay motionless beneath the bush, wishing the darkness and the storm away.

Daylight broke cold and gray, the trees still dripping endlessly. The wind drove the chill into his bones and left him weak and shaken, but by this time his mind was clear.

He began to think clearly, working out a plan.

The horses that were alive would have been driven off or taken by the outlaws. The water and a few hours' sleep gave him renewed strength. If he could get to his feet he might be able to walk.

He got his knife from its sheath on his belt and cut a willow stick an inch in diameter. Trimming off the branches, he used it to help him to stand. It bent dangerously as he put his weight on it, but it held, and he was able to pull himself erect. For a moment he stared about. The chuck wagon had been driven away so the food was gone but most of the drovers would have had hardtack or jerky in their saddlebags. There might even be something in his own.

Grimly he turned and hobbled in the direction of the roan he had been riding. It was all he could do to lower himself beside the horse and open the saddlebags. There was a small piece of jerky in the bag on top. He bit off a piece and stuffed the rest in his pocket.

Rafferty's horse lay on its side some distance away. There was no sign of the gambler's body. He might have been killed or he might have run away. That was the sort of thing he would have expected from the wizened, hard-featured cardsharp. He knelt painfully beside the dead mount and went through the saddlebags. There were two pieces of jerky and a derringer with a dozen bullets. John took the small gun, secreted it in a pocket, and sprawled there long enough to eat one piece of jerky. Then he pulled himself to his feet with the help of the willow stick and started walking, one uncertain step at a time.

It was all he could do to keep erect, even on level ground, and he fell painfully across a clump of soap weed when he stubbed his toe on a buffalo chip. For a time he breathed heavily, regaining his breath before struggling to his feet again.

It was then that he heard a sound behind him, the soft murmer of moccasined feet on the new grass. He threw the willow stick from him and clawed at the Colt Peacemaker in the holster on his hip. The sudden move brought a wave of nausea and threw him off balance. He sprawled helplessly across a cactus and lay still, bracing himself for the blade of a knife in his back.

But it did not come.

The Indian knelt over him, touching the wound with a forefinger. Then he spoke to his companions in Cheyenne and they, too, knelt beside him. The youthful brave turned him on his back. "You are alive!" he exclaimed in English.

Breckenridge opened his eyes but said nothing.

"We take you with us."

John gritted his teeth and looked away. He was their prisoner. They were probably taking him to their camp to torture him. They often did that with whites unfortunate enough to fall into their hands. He eyed them evenly. They weren't going to get any satisfaction from seeing him cringe.

They brought a pony and were going to help him climb on the skinny paint. He motioned them away and tried to mount it himself, but in the end they had to pick him up and put him on the little stallion. The pain was excruciating, and he clenched the mane with his fingers to keep from falling. Once or twice he swayed as the blackness swept over him.

It was several miles to the Indian camp. The dogs and the kids heard them first and dashed out to greet them. The boys saw that Breckenridge was white and picked up stones to throw at him, but his Indian captors saw what they were about to do and quickly stopped them. The women were next, standing shoulder to shoulder along either side of the path the Indian braves would follow. Then the men came out and stared at him. The braves left their lodges and stood silently and with great dignity, eyeing the captive.

Finally the young brave stopped John's horse at one of the larger, better-cared-for lodges. "But first I must talk to my father, Wounded Buffalo."

Breckenridge stirred weakly on the mount. He heard the voice of the youthful Indian and caught the reference to the chief, but that was all. He was again fighting to remain conscious.

Big Knife went into the lodge and consulted earnestly with his father. Wounded Buffalo nodded his approval. There was an evil gleam in the young brave's savage dark eyes when he returned. Breckenridge's life was being spared for now, for what reason John did not know. It could be to have sport with him later.

Root Digger, the young brave's mother, came to the opening and looked out, speaking sharply to the braves who had been with her son when they came across the badly wounded white man. She was a woman of authority. That was obvious. As she spoke they took him off the horse and carried him inside, laying him on a pile of skins.

Kneeling over him she cut away his shirt, exposing the angry, swollen flesh between his hip bone and ribs where the bullet had torn a jagged hole. She spoke sharply to one of her daughters. Red Deer went for water, brown feet flying along the path. Her younger sister built up the fire in the lodge and when the water was brought back put it on to heat.

Root Digger sponged away the dried blood and dirt from the ugly wound. As she did so the injury began to seep again. Bright red blood trickled from the wound. She was skilled in the treatment of such injuries and undisturbed by the badly infected bullet hole. The warm water caused the wound to bleed more profusely, and using the mashed roots of Curly Dock she made a poultice to help draw out the infection. Taking dried, powdered horsemint, she rubbed the substance over his body.

"For fever," she explained tersely when his eyes searched hers, questioning her actions. Then she made a brew of tea from some finely-crushed dried leaves. "Also for fever!" she said, as much for her daughters who needed to learn such things as her patient.

"Now," she said, "you go to sleep."

He nodded and closed his eyes. The last thing he remembered seeing was the withered old chief sitting cross-legged on the other side of the lodge, his sunken eyes glaring at him venomously.

It was some time the next day when John awakened. Root Digger, with Red Deer lingering silently nearby, cared for the young white man. She bathed the wound and changed the poultice. She had Red Deer boil a broth from the breasts of meadowlarks and feed him. This process was repeated day by day. He began to gain strength, bit by bit until he was strong enough to feed himself.

As Breckenridge began to recover he was able to piece together the events that led up to the battle that ended with most of the drovers being killed and the cattle driven away. The memory of the incident became more clear, and hatred burned within him. Kramer was the one responsible. He had to be! He had planned the second attack and had executed it ruthlessly, not caring how many deaths he caused.

But Breckenridge hadn't finished with him. He was going to find his former partner, no matter how long it took. The cattle would be gone. But he was going to give him what was coming to him if it took ten years!

For some reason Elihu's Bible came to mind. It had been in his other saddlebag, so it was gone.

Breckenridge began to feel a little better but was slow in regaining his strength. For several weeks he scarcely left the lodge, content to sit or lay in one corner watching Root Digger and her daughters cook and sew. After a time he was able to go outside, leaning heavily on the cane that had been given him.

On those occasions he made his way along the path, stopping now and then to watch the boys playing in the dust or the older women sitting in the shade of a "squaw cooler," working the green hides they were tanning. The younger women cared for their children and mended and sewed, talking endlessly.

There were those who were wives of the same Indian man. Usually they were sisters since the men believed that sisters got along better with each other in such a relationship than those from different families. Even then the husband kept each wife and her children in a separate lodge, not wanting to risk the problems of having them together.

The unmarried girls were kept close to their

mothers, learning the tasks that would be so important for them when they were married and set up homes in their husband's lodges. They were taught to tan hides, to make robes and clothes, and to pack the travois to move camp. They gathered firewood and cooked and helped take care of their younger brothers and sisters.

The older men smoked and gossiped while the younger, more energetic braves fashioned the tools they needed for wars and hunting. They made bows and arrowheads, shaping hunting and war heads from carefully chosen flint. And they all talked of the hated white men who were rolling in a great flood across the land.

They knew that John was picking up their language in his time with them and that he understood much of what they said. He was virtually well by this time, and he chafed to be on his way but knew this was impossible—at least for the moment. He had to wait until he was certain he was able to succeed before he made a try. To attempt escape and be caught would be disastrous.

The heat of summer that marked the month of the Moon When the Buffalo Bulls Are Rutting finally came to an end. The month of the Cool Moon was upon them when the tribe moved again. This time it was necessary for them to go to another hunting area where the game was more plentiful—a place where they could get their winter's supply of meat and skins for clothes and blankets. The Freezing Moon was only weeks away. When it arrived with the wind and cold and snow they would have to be in their winter hunting grounds.

As the winter drew close Breckenridge felt

the old power returning to his body. He was soon strong enough to move on and mentioned it several times to the young warrior who had found him and brought him to the Cheyenne village. But the Indian passed it off. It was not time for him to go yet, he said. Breckenridge knew what he meant, although it was never put into words. John was a prisoner of the Cheyenne. It was a still a benevolent sort of captivity. He had the run of the camp and when they moved he rode with the braves as one of them, but he knew he dare not try to leave.

Big Knife came regularly to see him. He sat cross-legged, across from the white man, studying his lean features and asking about the guns the drovers used. He and his companions had found two of the new repeating Winchester .76's the frontiersmen described as "the rifle you can load on Sunday and shoot all week." He wanted to know about them and particularly where they could get such weapons and ammunition.

Then John knew why he had been spared. They had found the guns and were determined to use him to get more such weapons for themselves.

Breckenridge hesitated. The new rifles were carefully kept out of the Indians' hands. The old Spencers and Henrys were formidable enough in the possession of hostiles. The Winchesters would give the warriors the firepower that could make them devastating on the warpath.

"The man I worked for furnished the rifles," he explained.

Big Knife leaned forward, his firm young face serious. "You get for us?" he asked.

John wouldn't lie to him about the weapons but he didn't want to refuse outright either. To do

108

so might trigger reprisals that could mean his life. "It is hard to get such guns," he hedged. "It is very hard."

"You had them," he said simply. "You get more. So we can shoot, *bang—bang—bang*. Get plenty buffalo. Plenty deer and elk."

"They cost much money."

There was a change in Big Knife's attitude, as though the negotiations had taken a decisive turn. "We pay. Much beaver! Much furs! You get rifles. We buy."

Big Knife's eyes narrowed and suspicion marred his dark features. Breckenridge could no longer ignore the Indian's persistent search for answers.

"The Great White Father does not want everyone to have such guns. He is afraid there will be trouble!" There! It was out—the reason for not getting the Cheyenne the Winchesters.

The Indian's face went livid with rage. "You not live, maybe! We kill, maybe!" he snarled.

"They are not mine to give."

The Indian brave was not satisfied with his explanation. Anger and suspicion lurked in Big Knife's eyes. He got to his feet and stormed out, almost knocking Root Digger down as he rushed from the lodge.

John watched uneasily until he was out of sight. Then he turned and leaned back on the blankets, closing his eyes.

Red Deer had seen all that had taken place. "It is a bad thing that he wants those guns," she said quietly. "It is so he will be a big man in the tribe. So he can ride at the head of the braves and count coup on the white man."

He opened his eyes and sat up. As his gaze

109

met hers she flushed and looked away. For the first time he noted the delicate cut to her features and her smooth, even, olive complexion.

"Your brother is an important man in the tribe," he said quietly.

"His heart burns to be the chief in the place of our father," she whispered. "Our mother, Root Digger, and I fear for what might happen."

12

The tribe moved from their summer grounds to the hills where there was plenty of wood for their fires and protection from the storms that would soon be raging. For weeks the hunters had been out every day, combing the canyons for game. The meat had been dried, the hides tanned, and the roots and food plants gathered and stored. By the time the first snows hid the ground and ice glistened on the ponds, the Cheyenne were as ready as they ever were for the hard months of winter.

There was a certain forboding among the people, however—an uneasiness that always came with the uncertainty brought by the cold. What if the storms were so severe the animal herds drifted with the wind to more friendly climes? What if the snow was so deep the deer and elk had trouble finding food to eat and starved or were caught and killed by the coyotes and wolves? It was a time when the harsh realities of nature weighed heavily on the Cheyenne.

While the older women worked on the hides, fashioning robes and clothing, the girls were sent out to gather wood, piling it close to the lodges of their fathers. Breckenridge, who was given nothing to do, walked idly about the camp, watching

111

what went on and chafing to be away—to start the search for Kramer and Rafferty, if the gambler was still alive.

He had done a great deal of thinking about Rafferty. He had an uneasy feeling about him. It had been with him since the gambler first won the herd and they started traveling together. They hadn't been on the trail long when he had seen the deceptiveness and the streak of cowardice in the card handler. Of course Rafferty could have been killed in the fight for the cattle, but he might also have slipped away when the battle was over. It might take months—even years—but he would find both Kramer and the gambler.

As time went on the weather grew colder and more threatening. Finally the clouds came up, hiding the sun. They provided an even, threatening slate-gray cover that reached from horizon to horizon. The wind was gusty, chilling to the bone. It whipped a few stray flakes of snow, fine as dust, across the path that led to the camp and tore the smoke from the tops of the lodges. Breckenridge pulled his coat collar up about his ears and turned toward the bevy of girls who were bringing in wood.

Red Deer was among them, her load larger than the rest. She was easily the most beautiful and graceful of the lot. He moved to one side and waited for them to pass. As they drew close one of the girls spoke softly to Big Knife's sister and her cheeks darkened. Flustered, she stumbled and sprawled on the hard ground, her load of wood scattering.

Breckenridge went quickly to her and knelt to examine her ankle.

"I'm all right," she protested, struggling to her feet in embarrassment.

"Let me carry the wood for you." He picked it up and started toward her father's lodge. Disapproval gleamed in her eyes but she was too shy to speak. A moment later Big Knife came around the corner of a lodge and saw them together.

He strode forward angrily, grabbed the wood from Breckenridge and slammed it into his sister's arms so savagely she almost went down again. "Touch her one more time and I'll kill you!"

John's temper flared. He was about to retort hotly, when he saw that half a dozen hostile young braves were watching sullenly, hoping he would do something stupid like challenging Big Knife. One unguarded move and he would have a tomahawk in his back or a club alongside his head.

"I was only doing for her what I would want someone to do for my sister if the same thing happened to her."

Big Knife scarcely heard him. "Our women are not like the Arapahoes. They don't sleep with any man who takes the notion! And we see that they stay that way!"

"I understand," Breckenridge retorted.

"I'll carve your heart out and feed it to the dogs if you don't leave Red Deer alone!" With that Big Knife whirled and stormed away, leaving Breckenridge to think about what had almost happened. He rejoined his companions, fury still twisting his dark features. They glared openly at him and muttered under their breath, but no one spoke directly to him.

In the lodge that night Red Deer watched Breckenridge until she realized that her brother

113

was eyeing her suspiciously. Her cheeks flushed and she turned away. Big Knife spoke to their father and padded out of the lodge. A cold blast of air surged in behind him as he rushed into the night.

John read the sudden fire in the young brave's glaring and was careful to avoid looking in Red Deer's direction from then on. She, too, was careful not to show interest in him. Instead, she acted as though he was no longer there, directing her attention to her parents and her younger sister.

Winter arrived on the teeth of a nasty wind that piled snow deep among the lodges. Once it came it did not let up. By the time Big Hard Face Moon gave way to Hoop and Stick Game Moon a scarcity of food hit the tribe. The roots and plants, so carefully husbanded, had long since been used and the meat was virtually gone.

Parents ate one meal a day and pretended they weren't hungry so their children would have enough. The food that was usually given so freely to guests was provided grudgingly. It was still provided because that was the custom of the tra- dition-minded Cheyenne, but there was resent- ment, thinly veiled from the occasional guests. The braves were devoting most of their time to hunting, except when the weather was too cold or the snow too deep.

Breckenridge knew the scarcity of game and ate as little as possible. On several occasions John suggested that he go hunting with the men, but they ignored him as they might a woman who had the temerity to suggest that she could take a man's place on the hunt or warpath. Finally, how- ever, he called the chief's ambitious son aside and informed him that he was going on the next hunting expedition.

"And if I say, 'no!'—what then?"

"I am good with a rifle," the white man informed him without answering directly. "I will get game! Food for the people!"

Big Knife's cheeks were dark with anger and his eyes flashed. "We will see how good you are!" he exploded. Turning to one of the others he ordered him to give John the Winchester he was carrying. "You will stay beside me!" the chief's son ordered. "If you try to run away I will kill you!"

"Your people have cared for me when I was not able to care for myself. You have given me food when you have had little. You have given me space in your lodge out of the cold and snow. I am an honorable man! I want to help you and your people!"

The chief's son spat contemptuously in the snow. "The white man is as honorable as the snake that crawls on its belly."

Breckenridge glared at him but did not reply.

They mounted their ponies and rode slowly, single file, through the snow in the direction of the hills. The cold was increasing in intensity as they made their way up the steep slopes. The drifts were deeper and more difficult to plow through than Breckenridge had figured on. It was all the wiry little ponies could do to push through the drifts to the top of the ridge.

The hours dragged slowly by and John felt himself weakening. Although he thought he had long since recovered from his wound, he realized now that he was still not as strong as he should be. His Indian companions traveled in silence. On the crest of the first ridge they stopped, surveying the slopes below. They were about to go on when John grasped Big Knife by the arm and pointed below. The brave jerked angrily away and grabbed for the blade in his belt. But John pointed out several white shapes, just discernable in the snow. He counted them. Three—four—six—seven mountain sheep feeding quietly on tender aspen branches.

Excitement gripped the hunters and two men raised their antiquated rifles to shoot. Breckenridge stopped them with a warning hand. They knew how far their bows and arrows could kill and they were clever at the art of tracking to get close enough to their game to make the kill, but rifles were new to them. They didn't fully recognize the differences between guns or the difficulty of shooting straight at longer distances. John checked the ammunition in the new-style Winchester they allowed him to use and, motioning for the others to stay behind, took Big Knife with him. They dismounted, tied their ponies to the nearest junipers, and set out, plowing through waist-deep snow. The two men inched forward cautiously, one careful step at a time.

By now it was late afternoon. The sun was sliding beneath the clouds that continued to spit snow, and a haze settled over the slope. Once or twice the lead buck looked up startled, and for an agonizing moment John was afraid the wily old sheep would sound a warning and charge away with the ewes close behind. Then, apparently satisfied that all was well, the wary animal turned back to the aspen once more, nibbling the branches as far up as he could reach.

The two men continued slowly until they

were within a hundred yards of their quarry. Fortunately the wind was blowing in their faces, giving the animals no warning scent. Carefully Breckenridge raised the rifle, squinted along the barrel, and fired. Almost at the same time Big Knife did the same. John levered shells into the barrel as rapidly as he could and shot. The buck got away but the other six sheep were killed, blood staining their white wool and the snow.

There was a feast in camp that night, followed by much dancing and singing and the sounds of drums. John knew the people were aware that he had been responsible for the hunt's success, but he was still a hated enemy—one they looked upon with contempt.

Everyone ate well that night and the next and the next. A new sense of expectancy took hold of the people. Now that things had turned for them, they reasoned the favorable circumstances would continue. The sense of dread gave way to an exuberant optimism.

The weather, as though deciding to cooperate, moderated, and the hunting parties were able to go out again. This time the Indians came and ordered Breckenridge to go with them. That hunt and the next were unsuccessful, but on the third they came across two bull buffalo and a cow, spending the winter in a canyon beyond the place where they killed the sheep. Again Big Knife joined John in stalking the huge, shaggy animals. They made their way down the mountainside, concealing themselves behind the juniper and aspen. Big Knife, anxious to make the first kill, shot before John was ready and the clumsy animals charged off. Firing faster than he had ever shot a rifle before, Breckenridge knocked down two of

117

the big animals. Big Knife got the third.

When they returned triumphantly to camp John decided the time had come to approach the Cheyenne about allowing him to leave. He called the chief's son to one side. "I have stayed with you for many moons," he began. "Your mother, Root Digger, brought me back to health and you and your sisters have become like family to me."

Big Knife frowned. "We will talk of it no more."

"We must talk! Now my heart aches for my own people. I would leave and go to my own."

Fury darkened the young brave's features. "You stay with us! We will hear no more about the matter!"

John hesitated. He was in a difficult situation. He had to plan, to work things out. To attempt to bull his way through could be disastrous. From that moment on he had one thought foremost in mind. He had to wait and plan, looking for the right time to escape.

As the weather moderated, the snow began to pack and melt. The hunters set snares, and they were soon catching rabbits and birds to augment the buffalo meat of the last big hunt. Another winter was safely behind them.

Spring Moon came and with it the first green grass showed in patches as the drifts melted. The white man's wagons began to move once more and the talk around the campfires grew ugly as the old men lamented the days of their fathers and the young men chafed at the thought of defeat—of being driven deeper and deeper into isolated corners of the land they called their own.

The drums talked late into the night and the war songs were sung, songs of fighting the enemy and counting coup and taking many horses—and many captives. The battles of the past were re-lived in minute detail, each storyteller embellishing his favorite account with new details, brewed in a fertile imagination.

The old women added to the stories, relating the tales of bygone days, keeping alive the part women had played in many of the great battles of the past. They told of their grandmothers encouraging the men of the tribe and urging the braves to fight.

Spring was also a time for love among the Cheyenne, a time for the choosing of mates and marriages. And true to the old traditional ways, the girls refused to consider the advances of the men who had not been tested in battle. A young man who had never been on the warpath was still a boy and no man at all.

And so the talk continued.

It might have remained just that, however, had the story of a raid by the hated horse soldiers not come into camp. A motley gang of Arapahoe hostiles rode in one evening, their ponies lathered and their faces twisted with hatred. The horse soldiers had been ordered out to exact punishment because a band of renegades like themselves had killed a couple of settler's cows. The troops found the nearest Arapahoe camp to teach the people a lesson. Women and children and old men had been killed, visiting every lodge in the camp with death. Something had to be done, the Arapahoe said ominously, or the horse soldiers would wipe out all the Indian people—the Cheyenne as well as the Arapahoe.

The outlaw Indians moved on the next morning, but their foul seed had been sown. Big Knife and his braves had been spoiling for a fight. Now they were determined to go on the warpath. The voices of the chanters and the drums were heard far into the night. The dances were more frantic than before.

Breckenridge noticed a difference in the way he was treated as well. Earlier he had the run of the camp. Now he was ordered away from places where the men were gathering. People who had been friendly earlier shunned him now, and boys threw stones when they saw him. Time, for him, was rapidly running out.

He still had the loaded derringer he had taken from Rafferty's saddlebag. Somehow he had managed to hide it from Big Knife and the others. But such a weapon would be as worthless as a slingshot if he was surprised trying to escape. And the bigger weapons were guarded carefully. He would have almost no chance of getting within a hundred yards of them—and even less chance of stealing one.

By this time the braves were sending out scouting parties, looking for whites they might attack. John waited and watched but with an affected carelessness, as though he was not aware of anything unusual going on and as though he had no thought of escaping.

Then Big Knife's most trusted friend rode into camp at breakneck speed, his mount lathered. From a distance John saw the rider rush inside. A few moments later half a dozen others sped off to spread the news: a party of horse soldiers was on patrol in the vicinity. This was what they had been waiting for! This was the opportunity to hit the horse soldiers, to make them pay for what they had done to the Arapahoes. John realized that this was different than anything he had seen in his months with the Cheyenne.

Almost immediately, war paint was being applied and the women began to sing and dance. One by one the braves were ready for battle. John was sent back to the lodge of Wounded Buffalo where he was securely tied.

"Until tomorrow," Big Knife whispered, grinning evilly, "then you can join us!"

"Not against my own people!" the captive white man announced firmly.

"You will have one choice! Fight with us or be killed!"

13

John Breckenridge lay motionless on the skins in the far corner of Wounded Buffalo's lodge. His feet were securely fastened with rawhide and his wrists were tightly bound behind his back. The darkness of night had settled in—an opaque blackness so thick it hid the outer reaches of the lodge. All he could see were the shapeless forms of the family's few belongings. The medicine bag that Root Digger used in caring for the sick and injured was hanging from the center pole and the few clothes they had were along one side. He could not have recognized anything in the inky shadows had he not known what each bump was.

The war dance was building in fury. The fierce tattoo of the drums increased and the tempo of the beat picked up measurably. New voices were added to the din—wild, frenzied voices that revealed the building emotion of the dancers.

While the dance and the war songs were going on, Wounded Buffalo and his council returned to the chief's lodge, built up the fire, and sat around it. They saw their white captive in the corner but ignored him as though he was another buffalo robe. The aged chief took the pipe, lighted it with great dignity, took two or three shallow puffs, and passed it to the old man to his left.

"The young men are anxious to go to war to avenge the deaths of our Arapahoe brothers," the chief said quietly. "They think we are too old for war—too cautious and too much afraid of death."

"Big Knife and his braves have 'painted their robes' four times this spring," an elder added. "Before the cottonwood buds began to swell they were four times on raiding parties, stealing ponies and counting coup. Now they think they are beyond such things. They are determined to lead the band into battle."

Breckenridge listened intently.

"Big Knife wants to 'carry the war pipe' in this affair."

"Is he wise enough to lead men in such a battle?" one of the old ones asked. "Does he know he must pray to the arrows to gain their favor? Can he sense an ambush and take the enemy without losing too many of his own men?"

The men waited in silence, staring into the fire, each wrapped in his own thoughts.

"The women are urging revenge," an old and trusted warrior observed at last. "They want the white man's horse soldiers to pay for the blood they have spilled."

Wounded Buffalo was their chief. For more years than they could count they had followed his leading, going to war when he said it was time, remaining at peace when the spirits warned him against going to war. Now they looked to him for counsel. They waited while he reached for the pipe, held it in his hand for a time, then puffed on it thoughtfully. "If the signs are right," he said, "it is a time for war."

Murmers of assent circled the little group.

"My son came to me this morning with the

pipe, asking to take the braves into battle,"
Wounded Buffalo acknowledged. "I told him to
make an offering to the medicine arrows so he
could know their wishes."

"Did he do it right?" one of the council asked.
It wasn't enough to do the right things at the right
times. They had to be done properly. "Were his
gifts acceptable?"

"He put on his buffalo robe with the hair side
out. He took his gift for the arrows and a pipe of
tobacco and went to the lodge of the arrows."

"I saw and heard him," another said approv-
ingly. "You would have been proud. The spirits
could find no fault in him. After the gifts were
blessed he bundled them and prayed to the arrows, telling them he was going out with the
young men to take many scalps and punish the
horse soldiers for their crimes against the Arapahoe. He wanted to take many horses and kill many
white men. He wanted his braves to come back to
the camp happy and with blackened faces. The
arrow-keeper smoked with him. . . . All was in
order."

Still, there was disagreement among the
council. Some felt that the chief's son was much
too young—too impetuous and lacking in experience. They thought Wounded Buffalo and the
rest of the council should go along, taking charge
of the strategy. Others were discouraged and
weary of the burden they had been carrying.

"Our skin is wrinkled and our eyes are dim,"
Wounded Buffalo's most trusted adviser said.
"The strength is gone from our legs and I am
afraid we lack the will to make war. Better it is
that we allow others to do what we can no longer
do for our people." And so the discussion went on

while the noise of the war dance grew louder and more frenetic.

The chief breathed deeply. "While we wait and talk we are losing our opportunity to hold the land."

"And the white man who is with us?" someone else asked.

"He goes with Big Knife," Wounded Buffalo said venomously. "If he does not fight, he dies!"

"And maybe he dies anyway," one of the others added sagely.

The old men passed the pipe from one to the other, solemnly smoking it. Then they returned it to Wounded Buffalo, who put it away as they filed out. No one glanced in John's direction.

For a time after they left he struggled against the thongs that held him, but Big Knife had tied him securely. Straining against the rawhide he was able to move his feet and hands slightly, but not enough to wriggle free.

Closing his eyes he lay back while he listened to the drums and the toneless chanting of the dancers. If he was to get away from the Cheyenne it would have to be done now, while they were still in the village. Once he rode off with the war party he would be watched too closely to make a move.

But how? *How?*

He didn't hear the flap·on the lodge open or the soft footsteps approaching.

"S–Sh!" a gentle voice whispered softly in his ear. "Don't make any noise!"

He opened his eyes quickly. The fire that had been built up by the council earlier cast eerie shadows on the skin walls of the lodge. He looked up into the smooth, olive features of Big Knife's sister. "Red Deer!"

She put a warning finger to her lips. "They would kill us both if they knew I was here."

"Why did you come?" he demanded, the words harsh in his throat.

"You have had only good will toward our people," she whispered. "You have been kind to our people. You killed game for us when we were hungry. I have talked with our mother. She agrees that it is not our way to reward kindness with evil. Turn so I can untie you."

He did as he was told. "Did anyone see you come here?" he demanded.

"They are all busy with their dancing and their war songs," she answered. "Big Knife will think he didn't tie you well."

Hurriedly she loosed the thongs.

"The horse soldiers are in the hills," she whispered. "Big Knife sang a song about them. So that is where he will lead the braves. Take a pony and ride to the plains! Quick! Before someone thinks to check on you."

The instant the rawhide was undone, Breckenridge got to his feet, rubbing his wrists to get the circulation going again.

"I have this for you," she whispered, handing him one of the Winchester rifles.

He nodded seriously.

For a moment John stared down at the slight form of the Indian girl. Then he touched her arm. She was trembling with emotion and for the first time he realized how frightened she was and the risk she was taking to save his life. "Red Deer," he whispered, "I will never forget you!" With that he was gone, slipping noiselessly out of the lodge toward the place where the horses were tethered.

The war dance was still occupying the attention of the people. They were caught up in the frenzy of the beating drums and the songs that had stirred the hearts of the Cheyenne for untold generations. There might be wailing in the camp come nightfall, but now their hearts were awakened and they were again a proud, unconquerable nation.

Breckenridge stole swiftly down the steep slope to the makeshift remuda where the Indian ponies were held. He would have only moments in which to get away.

There was always the unexpected to betray him. The ever-present dogs might pick up his scent and set up a cry that echoed above the drums and the singing, or one of the ponies might snort as he approached the remuda. If it came at a lull in the music he would be heard. Or Big Knife might see Red Deer returning to the crowd and become suspicious enough to go and check Wounded Buffalo's lodge.

John dashed down to the ponies and selected one of the biggest and strongest. He was a big man, and the ponies the Cheyenne rode were small and thin. The strength of his mount could make the difference between being caught and getting away. He led the pony a short distance from the others, slipped an Indian bridle on the half-wild animal, vaulted to its back, and stole silently away. He was counting on Big Knife's burning ambition to keep the young Indian from trailing him even after he discovered John was missing. There was no name to be made for himself by searching out a lone white man, hated though he was.

Quietly he rode away from the remuda down

the narrow game trail. He crossed the open area where the boys played their games, forded the stream where the women went for water, and angled in the direction of the narrow valley. He listened intently for evidence that someone in the Cheyenne camp had missed him, but there was no sign of an outcry.

As Breckenridge continued to ride away from the village, the sounds grew fainter until he could no longer hear the drums and the discordant chanting. With all quiet once again, he jabbed his heels into the Indian pony's flanks and the valiant little paint plunged into a hard gallop. John kept him at top speed until he heard a change in the pony's labored breathing. He pulled him down to a brisk walk.

By daylight he had reached the valley and found the trail that led to Fort McClellan. If there was a patrol in the hills they should be warned of the impending raid.

He found a small water hole near the trail where he stopped, dismounted, and let the pony drink and rest. Shading his eyes with his hands, he studied the route he had just traveled. There was no sign that anyone was behind him. Sprawling on the ground, he closed his eyes and dozed for a time while his mount grazed. An hour later he mounted again and continued up the trail, this time at a slower, less punishing pace.

It was shortly before noon when he reached the first sign of habitation—a ramshackle set of ranch buildings some distance from the trail. He turned toward the weathered house with broken shutters and a roof that must have leaked.

He was some forty yards from the house when a grizzled old woman stepped out of the kitchen door, a battered Henry rifle at her shoulder. "That's far enough, mister! Don't come no closer or I'll shoot!"

"I came to warn you! There's going to be trouble with the Cheyenne!" he shouted.

The old lady's expression did not change. At that instant an old man several years her senior joined her.

"He's all right, woman!" he exclaimed, spitting a stream of tobacco juice onto the ground to one side of the broken steps. "He ain't Indian!"

"Then what's he doing with that there horse?"

"Don't talk to *me* about it!" he snarled. "He's got a mouth! Ask him!"

Breckenridge dismounted. "If you'll put that Henry gun away, I'll tell you," he said.

John made his way to the ramshackle, broken-down porch and told them how he had been taken captive by the Cheyenne. "Now they're fixing to go on the warpath," he concluded, "so when I got away I started riding for the fort, fast as this critter could carry me."

Long before he had finished, the old woman accepted what he was saying. She put aside the rifle and invited John in to eat with them. "Like as not, you ain't had a decent meal since them savages found you. Come in and set! I'll fix some proper food. Something that'll stick to your ribs!"

Before leaving their place he had the best meal he had eaten in months, bought a horse from them, and got the loan of a saddle and bridle, which he was to leave at the fort for them to pick up the next time they went in.

"You can take that Injun horse with you," the old man said. "I don't want them savages to get the idea I stole it. A man's got his reputation to think of."

"You'd best come in to the fort with me," Breckenridge urged. "There's no telling how far those savages'll range. They could cause plenty of trouble."

The old man, gnarled as a spike of mesquite and bushy as greasewood, squinted sourly at his wife. "I know what I'm a mind to do. How about you, woman?"

"We ain't let no Indians run us out so far," she said, a grin cracking her toothless mouth. "This ain't no time to start."

"I lived with those people," John protested. "Big Knife is bad medicine! He's got it in his head he's going to be chief and he's fixing to prove himself the toughest, orneriest Indian brave in these parts."

The old man grinned again. "Me and ma are of a mind to stay here and look after things the way we've always done. Right, woman?"

She nodded grimly.

"Those savages are out for blood," John said.

"If they come looking for trouble, we ain't exactly going to be sitting around."

He waved to them and rode off, leading the Indian pony behind him.

14

When Breckenridge was several miles from the ranch he paused long enough to free the Indian pony. Cracking the wiry pinto on the rump with a rope, he sent him galloping over the prairies.

After a time he reined in the hammerhead roan he had bought from the old rancher and surveyed the bleak prairie. He saw no sign of anyone on the trail or on the bleak, barren grasslands that stretched from the horizon on the east to the hills that mounted to the western sky. The sun blazed across the afternoon sky and was plunging behind the hills when he cantered up to the fort and through the open gates.

The commanding officer was a serious young man, a recent graduate from West Point and very determined to do a good job. He was most concerned that the Cheyenne were giving trouble. "We've had some problems with the Arapahoe and the Sioux," he said, "but the Cheyenne have been quiet since I got out here in September." He came around the corner of his battered desk. "I was hoping they would stay that way."

"Not this bunch. They've had a rough winter. Now they're ill-tempered and spoiling for a fight."

The CO went over to the map on the wall and studied it for a time. "I've got a detachment right about here," he said, pointing to the mountains near the Cheyenne winter camp.

"Big Knife and his boys are on the prowl in those hills."

"Think we can warn them?"

"Could be—if they haven't tangled already."

The CO summoned an aide and gave orders to have a detachment ready to leave in an hour. Once that was done he motioned Breckenridge to a chair and sat down wearily himself. "I want to do a good job out here. But it's not easy." He hesitated for a moment. "Everybody's got a different idea of what ought to be done. The rancher wants to keep the Indian from stealing his stock. The settlers want them held down tight enough so they don't kill anybody and don't burn any houses or barns or destroy any crops. Like I said, it's not easy."

Breckenridge studied the youthful face.

"I had a problem a couple of weeks ago," the officer went on. "I was in Denver on army business when a rancher north of here lost a couple of steers to a party of hostiles. My acting CO let the guy talk him into sending out a platoon to find and punish the braves who were guilty—Arapahoes, I think."

"I heard about it."

"He got his revenge on a camp of women and old men and kids." Bitterness crept into the youthful voice. "I stripped him of his command and shipped him out, but I caught thunder from most of my officers and the people who live around here. They don't want to treat these Indian people like they're human."

"You've got a point."

He smiled. "One of these ranchers has a

brother in Congress in Washington. He's been writing letters back East. Now it looks as though I'm the one who's going to get investigated. Two senators and a congressman are on their way out here to look into my conduct. I may be relieved of my command."

When the detachment of soldiers was ready to leave the fort, John volunteered to go along. "I may be able to save them some time."

The horse John bought from the grizzled old rancher wasn't much of a mount for a man his size. He talked with the captain and was directed to a settler who had reached the fort several weeks before. The man and his family were waiting for someone heading back east. He sold him a broad-backed stallion to replace the roan and a proper saddle and bridle.

John led the soldiers out of the fort. It would have been easier to follow the trail, at least until they reached the hills, but it was half a day's ride out of the way. Half a day might mean the difference between life and death for the platoon.

By nightfall Breckenridge and the soldiers had crossed the prairie and reached the hills to the west. He kept them moving until darkness swallowed the trail and it was impossible to continue. They tethered their mounts in the thin mountain grass and spread out their bedrolls to sleep.

Shortly after midnight the moon came up. John had the sentry waken the men, and they were soon picking their way up the steep slope single file. They stopped briefly at daylight, had a cold breakfast of jerky, and made their way over the first ridge and down the other side. The sun arose presently, warming the riders and brightening their spirits.

John led the detachment as rapidly as he could without sapping the reserve strength of their mounts. They crossed a turbulent mountain stream swollen out of its banks by the early summer runoff, headed down a twisting canyon, and made their way up still another game trail to the top of the ridge. John reined in and studied the mountainside below. In a scattered stand of juniper he saw the soldiers. Some were lying on the ground and others were working with their horses.

A sudden ache gripped him. They were too late! The battle with Big Knife and his braves had already taken place! Waving the men to follow, he plunged down the mountain toward the site of the battle. When they were still some distance away he could see that the bodies of a number of Cheyenne braves were scattered among the trees, mingled indiscriminately with those of the cavalry.

"We gave 'em as good as we took, and maybe some better," the sergeant said laconically. "We saw they were going to ambush us and got out before they could close the trap."

Breckenridge covered the battleground, hoping he wouldn't find what he was looking for. But he did. Big Knife was sprawled grotesquely against a rock, an ugly red stain beginning to darken between his shoulder blades. He turned the body over as gently as possible. The chief's only male heir was still alive. Life was ebbing from him, but he opened his glazed eyes, recognizing the white man who bent over him.

"You!" Big Knife managed. Hate gave him strength he hadn't had before. For the moment it drove away the shock and pain.

"I came only to guide those who would warn the horse soldiers of your ambush."

"When we find you I not let the braves kill you!" he snarled. "I was a fool!"

John saw that his lips were parched. He took his canteen to give the Indian a drink—at least enough to moisten his mouth.

But Big Knife turned his head and clamped his lips tightly. "I want nothing from you!"

John did not speak. He knew only too well how the proud young brave would feel. His people had taken him in—had made him well. And he had repaid them with this.

"You talk Red Deer into freeing you," the dying Indian accused hotly. "On the way I figure it out. I thought she was with Walking Bear. They have eyes for each other. Only Walking Bear not leave war dance. Finally I see what happen!"

John's heart spasmed. "Does anybody else know?" he demanded, fearful for the girl's safety.

Big Knife closed his eyes. When he opened them he was much weaker, but the hatred was still there.

His lips curled. "I tell no one! I want to punish her myself! I want to take her by the throat and choke the life from her! She does not deserve to live!"

His head turned to one side and his body went limp. He was dead.

For a time Breckenridge held Big Knife in his arms. He stared down at the features, still filled with hate even in death.

"Know him?" one of the soldiers asked quietly.

"I knew him," he replied.

"It's tough to lose a friend, even an Indian."

John looked up. "I don't know that I could call him a friend. He'd have killed me if he'd gotten the chance."

The soldiers rode off in the direction of the fort, but Breckenridge did not stay with them. He had places to go and things to do. Things like getting a line on Kramer.

As John rode away he looked back at Big Knife's body, thinking for a moment of the proud young man who was lying there and the grief Root Digger and Red Deer would experience.

The Cheyenne would not leave the bodies of the fallen braves more than a few hours. When the time passed for them to have returned the old men would sit in council. The deliberation would end by sending out a detachment of older, more cunning braves, charged with finding out what had happened. They would find the bodies and take their dead back to the camp where there would be wailing and bitter talk against the horse soldiers.

He rode south, skirting the territory where the Cheyenne were camped, and headed for the trail that would lead him back to the route the trail herds followed.

To be sure, the trail he was seeking was a year old, but cattle herds were events in the lives of the people who were trying to eke a living from the hard, dry soil and those who lived in the little towns along the route. If he saw enough people and asked enough questions he might be able to get answers. His heart hardened as he thought about Kramer and his men. They had caused some good men to be killed—some very good men, like Cookie, whom everybody liked. They were going to have to pay for that.

John directed his attention to the task ahead. He rode across the hills and into a valley toward the nondescript town where he and Rafferty had last bought supplies. It was a ragtag collection of houses and saloons and the assortment of stores that were necessary to meet the needs of the people.

He went to the general store where he dipped deeply into his small horde of gold to buy a new six-gun—a Colt Peacemaker like the one the Indians had taken from him. He also bought cartridges, a few supplies, and a pair of saddlebags. Then he began to ask about the herd.

The storekeeper, a paunchy individual with scraggly gray hair forming a ragged horseshoe around the sides and back of his shiny pate, professed to remember Breckenridge, but there was a blank look in his eyes that gave him away. "I couldn't forget you, now could I?" he exclaimed, managing a thin laugh. "You brought your chuck wagon in and filled up with beans and ham and bacon and . . . let's see." He scratched his head. "Let's see. You got flour and Arbuckle Coffee."

"Have you seen any of our men this spring?" John asked. "Anyone who was with us a year ago?"

That seemed to stop him. He put his pencil to one side with the bill half-figured and frowned. "I remember the cook. He came in here a couple of months ago with an order about as big as the one you gave me last spring."

A queer light gleamed in John's eyes.

"What's the matter?" the storekeeper demanded. "Don't you believe me?"

"Not about Cookie, I don't. He was killed a year ago."

The store owner flushed.

With that, Breckenridge paid him and gathered his supplies and grub. "I'm trying to find the man who stole our herd."

Recognition glittered in the older man's eyes. "I remember now!" he exclaimed. "It was quite a mess. Dead men and horses all over the place. I talked with the sheriff from over that way. He'd been out there soon after it happened." The storekeeper folded his arms on the counter and leaned on them. "Reckon you've got a chance of catching up to the scum what did it?"

"It may take a spell, but I'll catch them. And when I do, they'll be sorry they shot anyone or even laid a hand on one of them longhorns."

He left the store, put the saddlebags on the stallion, and led the animal over to the hitching rail in front of the nearest saloon. His Colt Peacemaker hung uncomfortably on his hip. It had been a year since he had carried such a weapon and it felt heavy and cumbersome.

It was late afternoon and the bartender was almost alone. He stirred as John strode through the swinging doors and made his way up to the bar.

"What'll you have? Beer?"

"Just a little information."

The bartender scowled. "There ain't no money in information."

Breckenridge grinned. "You don't look too busy to talk some."

"Depends on what it's about?"

"Remember that herd of longhorns that was jumped by outlaws north and west of here?"

"And if I do?"

"Did you ever hear what came of the herd and

the hombres that killed off the drovers and stole it?"

The barkeeper was silent. He took time to roll a cigarette and touch a match to the twisted end.

"Can't say that I have. All we heard was that it was a bloody mess. . . . Sorry."

John made the rounds of the saloons and the other businesses, questioning anyone who would talk to him. But if they knew anything they weren't talking. For all they would say, the outlaws dropped in out of nowhere, pulled off the raid, and disappeared with the herd the same way. But that didn't surprise him. He was just getting started. Somewhere in one of the towns or forts along the trail he would get a lead. Somebody who knew something would drop a hint of what had taken place and he would be on Kramer's trail. When that happened he would be on his way— taking the first hard steps on the trail that would lead him to the man who had been responsible for the deaths of the drovers and Cookie. It would take time, but he would be on the move. And he wouldn't stop until he had found the outlaws and made them pay for what they had done.

15

Breckenridge followed the trail Kramer had laid out before they left Texas, stopping at every town and relay station and fort to inquire about the herd and the men who stole it. He went to the saloons and general stores and livery stables, describing his former partner and asking about the herd. He talked with blacksmiths and peace officers and soldiers, searching for those who might remember the longhorns and the man who claimed to own them.

His efforts were unproductive and seemingly endless. The answers were the same. There had been a continual stream of cattle going north the year before and the drovers were all alike. They were hard-drinking, hard-riding Texans who stayed to themselves except when they hit town for a good time. Then they caused so much trouble everyone was sick of them by the time they moved on.

"Nobody in these parts wants to remember those outfits," a barber told John.

It was slow, discouraging work, but Breckenridge began to pick up bits of information.

"They were shot up pretty bad," a scrubby, hard-bitten squatter told him. "Said they'd been raided by a band of rustlers. Wanted to know if there was a doctor in these parts and someplace where they could pick up some more hands."

That was the best lead John had uncovered. "Is there a doctor around?" he asked.

"Over in Signal Point."

John thanked him and rode on. From an earlier drive he remembered the wide, rutted main street of Signal Point with its rows of shoddy, hastily-erected buildings on either side. Once there, he dismounted, tied his horse to the hitching rail, and went inside.

The doctor was busy with a boy who had broken his leg when a horse fell on him, and John had to wait. Finally the leg was taken care of and the doctor came out, wiping his hands. His face was wet with sweat, and moisture stained his shirt. He surveyed his guest critically. "You don't look sick to me!"

"I want to ask a few questions."

The doctor lowered his broad frame into a dilapidated old chair that had been wired together for strength in the long distant past. He pulled a soiled handkerchief from his pocket and mopped his features. "What makes you think this is the place to get your answers?"

"I was told you took care of some Texas cowmen who got shot up bringing their herd north."

The doctor acted as though he hadn't heard him.

"I don't know why I didn't stay in Philadelphia where I belonged," he muttered. "All I get done out here is delivering babies and patching up bullet holes and busted legs and arms. And what do I get for pay? A dozen eggs or a couple of chickens or a side of pork—if I'm lucky."

For a moment John was silent, trying to form

his questions carefully. "They tell me you've been doctoring here for quite awhile."

"Too long." He pulled himself erect.

"Do you recollect a big hombre coming in with some of his drovers? Claimed to have had a fight with rustlers who tried to make off with the herd?"

"Nope," the doctor retorted.

"You sure?"

He squinted narrowly. "Now I did have a guy come in with some shot-up drovers. Claimed it was an Indian raid they'd fought off." The doctor took a cigar from his pocket and rolled it thoughtfully between his thumb and forefinger.

John waited for him to continue.

"He said it had just happened a couple of days before and his cook took care of patching them up. But those wounds weren't made by the rifles I've seen Indians have. I thought at the time that the fight had to have been with men who could shoot." He paused significantly. "Whoever they tangled with knew what they were doing."

"Anything else you can tell me?"

"I could tell you more than you'd ever want to hear. This boss-man made out the fight had happened a couple of days before, but that wasn't so. It had been a week—maybe ten days. Infection really had a hold on the lot of them. One man died right in this office."

When the doctor finished talking he leaned back, lighted his cigar, and pulled the smoke into his lungs.

"Did he happen to say where he was heading?"

"As a matter of fact, he did. Told me they were on their way to Fort Andrews. He heard the

142

army was buying beef up that way."

John knew where Fort Andrews was. He had been on other drives that sold beeves there.

Another patient came in and John excused himself.

"If you stop by this way again," the doctor called after him, "come and see me. OK?"

There was a new commanding officer at Fort Andrews who knew nothing about Kramer and the cattle he tried to sell but he had a clerk check the records. There was a notation in the ledger that eight hundred head of longhorn had been bought for the fort. Half of that number were to be delivered to Fort Robinson.

Breckenridge found that his former partner had split off the beeves for the Nebraska installation and sent them there with one of the drovers in charge. He took the rest of the herd west himself.

John followed him to Denver where he learned that the herd had been disposed of, bringing a good price. Kramer had told the buyers that he would be back again the following year.

Wherever John went he also inquired about Rafferty. He described the gambler carefully but was unable to find out anything about him. Finally, satisfied that he could learn no more about either Kramer or Rafferty in the Denver area, he rode east to Fort Robinson where the cattle had been delivered. Unfortunately that proved to be a waste of time.

Then Breckenridge decided to go to Ogallala. It was a wild, wide-open settlement, the kind Kramer and his crew would like. But finding Kramer wasn't the only reason for detouring to the rowdy Nebraska town on the Platte. That was where Helen Norvall and her folks lived. It had been a long time since he had seen her. He had been thinking a lot about her lately, wondering if she would even remember him.

He rode into Ogallala from the north, cutting across the hills in the vast reaches of the blue stem country—land the Indians still feared and gave a wide berth. The rambunctious community had changed but little. Front Street was still roaring, and two new saloons had been opened along with another bank and a barber shop.

He went to the livery stable, made arrangements for them to take care of his mount, and was about to leave when he saw a familiar horse in one of the stalls—a rangy line-back dun with white stockings on the front feet. John turned to the hostler. "Nice-looking animal. Know who he belongs to?"

The ruddy-cheeked young hostler nodded. "The new gambler over to the Crystal Palace . . . Beautiful horse."

That horse was one of those John brought to the remuda when he threw in with Kramer. It was one he rode himself. "You say a gambler owns him?"

"Around here only a gambler or a gunslinger would have money enough to own a fine animal like that."

Breckenridge had intended to go to the barbershop to get cleaned up and head for the hotel Helen's parents operated. Seeing the dun, however, caused him to change his mind. He made his way to the Crystal Palace, pushing through the swinging doors.

It was early in the afternoon and the saloon was almost deserted. The bartender was leaning across the richly polished mahogany bar, talking to a couple of cowhands who had started drinking early. An overdressed saloon girl was sitting alone at a table, her garish, painted features making her appear incredibly alone and forlorn. She saw him looking at her and managed an inviting smile, but he turned away.

The first two rows of tables were empty but in the far corner a familiar figure sat at faro. Rafferty!

The gambler hadn't seen John. He adjusted the blue sunshade he wore and dealt to the two somber players across from him. He was resting his arms on the worn tabletop.

Breckenridge turned to the bartender. "How long's Rafferty been dealing faro here?"

"Rafferty?" His forehead crinkled. "There's no one here by that name."

"Who's that?" He motioned in the gambler's direction.

"New man. Calls himself Applegate. Phineas Applegate. He's a good one. Cool as ice. Hardly ever has trouble because someone loses."

Breckenridge sauntered over to the table. Rafferty knew someone was there, but didn't look around.

"Hello, Sam," he said quietly.

The gambler's head jerked up, and for an instant John was sure he was going for the derringer he carried in his sleeve.

"I wouldn't if I were you," he warned.

"You've got me mixed up with someone else," Rafferty blustered. "My name's Phineas—"

He would have continued but John cut him off. "I know your name. And I know that horse you've got over in the livery barn belongs to me."

145

Rafferty picked up the cards and motioned the gamblers away with a wave of his hand. "The table's closed. You'll have to come back."

"You can't do that!" the young cowhand stormed. "You've got to give us a chance to win back what we've lost."

"You'll have to come back," he repeated. "You've got shut of enough for one day."

The man cursed bitterly and jumped to his feet as though to reach across the table and grab the faro dealer by the throat, but the derringer leaped to the gambler's hand.

"I wouldn't try!"

The liquor-flushed face went white. "I–I'll be back in town in a couple of days. You have that faro deck warmed up."

When the youthful, would-be gamblers wove their way uncertainly among the tables and stumbled out the door Breckenridge pulled out a chair and sat down, his face an icy mask.

"It–It wasn't like it looked, John," the gambler began, stammering uncertainly. "I—"

"You ran out on us. You turned tail and ran!"

He swallowed hard. "I know it looks bad," he continued. "But that wasn't the way it was. I stayed and fought alongside the men until you and Cookie and the others were—" He stopped and started over. "When you were shot I–I figured there wasn't any use in letting them kill me, too." His voice raised plaintively. "I wanted to stay alive to get back at Kramer. I've been looking for them ever since."

Breckenridge nodded. "I see how hard you've been looking."

Sam Rafferty winced. "A feller's got to eat." He managed a weak smile. "I'd buy you a drink for

146

old time's sake, but I know you don't use the stuff." He put the cards away. "We could go over to the cafe and have a steak. I'll buy."

"I'm particular about who I eat with."

"I'm only trying to be friendly and sociable. But you make it tolerable hard."

John lowered his voice. "I want a bill of sale for that horse in the livery barn."

"He was in the remuda," Rafferty blustered. "He belongs to me."

"He's a horse I put there when I threw in with Kramer. He's mine! I'm going to have him."

"Can you prove that?"

Breckenridge grabbed the gambler by the shirt collar and hauled him half out of the chair. "I don't have to prove it!" he exclaimed.

"All right. All right. Take him!"

Without removing his gaze from Rafferty, John reached in his shirt pocket and removed a soiled piece of paper. "Write me a bill of sale!"

Defiance leaped to Rafferty's eyes. "I haven't got a pencil."

"Then get one! But don't try anything. One move toward that little gun in your sleeve and I'll blow you apart. Understand?"

"Have you forgot? We were friends! Partners!"

"I haven't forgotten but I think you have!" He motioned toward the bar. "Now let's get up real easy like and go up to borrow the bartender's pencil. But just remember. I'm right behind you with my hand on my gun!"

16

Rafferty wrote out a bill of sale and handed it to Breckenridge.

"I hope you're satisfied!"

John read the paper and threw it on the table in front of the faro dealer. "Date it," he ordered, "and sign it with the name you're using now and the one you went by when I knew you."

"You don't trust a guy much."

"You aren't much to trust, Sam," he retorted angrily. Breckenridge folded the paper with one hand and stuffed it into his pocket. "I'll tell the hostler you'll stop by to pick up the feed and care bill for the dun."

"You're wearing the gun."

"Want me to take it off?" he asked softly.

"There'll be another time, Breckenridge," he warned.

John stalked out, retraced his steps to the livery barn, showed the bill of sale to the hostler so he could claim the dun, and sold the horse he bought from the settler who was heading back home.

With the money he got clean underwear, a couple of shirts, and a new suit. It wasn't the best in the store but it would have to do. He was fortunate to have enough cash for that and still be able to buy his meals and pay the keep for the horse at the livery barn.

Excitement gripped him as he went to the barbershop, got a bath, a haircut, and a regular shop-bought shave. The barber was a garrulous individual who was harmless enough, but Breckenridge found his endless chatter an irritation.

"You're getting all duded up," he said. "Must have your eye on one of those new gals over to the Crystal Palace."

"Not so's you could notice," he said irritably.

"Then you must have a regular gal friend. You ain't the kind to get all dandied up on your own."

John did not answer him. He felt uncomfortable in the suit and the shirt with a stiff collar and narrow black tie. The new clothes were uncommonly warm in the August sun. It had been the first time in more than a year since he had dressed up. He had the uneasy feeling that everyone on the street was watching him.

He made his way to the far end of the second block and crossed Front Street to the hotel. It was strange how familiar everything was, as though he had only been gone a few days. The broken board he remembered in the front step had been repaired and the gold lettering on the plate glass window appeared to have been redone, but that was all. Everything else was just as he remembered. Would it be the same with Helen?

He paused at the door, straightened his tie, and stepped into the lobby. Matt Norvall was at the desk, bent over the books, and his wife, Rebecca, was dusting the captain's chairs. They heard him come in but must have thought he was a guest going up to his room. They did not glance up.

He cleared his throat. "Any chance of getting a place to stay?" he asked.

Rebecca stared at him. "John!" she exclaimed, running to him. "John Breckenridge!"

Matt came around the corner of the chest-high desk, a broad smile lighting his face. "You're a sight for sore eyes!"

Rebecca took both of his big, calloused hands in hers. "You don't know how many times we've talked about you, wondering where you were and what you were doing and if you'd ever come this way again."

He began to relax slightly. "I've been wanting to get back, but something always came up."

"You're here. That's the main thing." Then, as though just remembering her manners, she said, "We don't have to stand out here. Let's go back to the parlor."

"Better yet, we can go into the kitchen and have a cup of Becky's coffee and some doughnuts," Matt put in. "She just baked fresh this morning."

They went into the kitchen and sat down at the table that had been so familiar to him.

"Now, tell us all about yourself," Rebecca began, setting the doughnuts before him and pouring a cup of coffee.

"There's not much to tell." He paused momentarily. "How have you two been?" he asked. "And what about the girls?"

"Helen will be home any minute," Rebecca said. "And won't she be surprised!"

"I thought she might have gone off someplace

to work," he ventured, "or had a home of her own." That was as close as he could come to asking if there was another man in her life.

"She's had a few beaus coming around of a Saturday night, but she hasn't seemed to be too much interested in them. How about you? You didn't bring a wife along?"

"Me?" He was amazed at the relief that swept over him to learn that Helen was still unattached. "Nobody'd have me."

Matt was called to the front desk and when he finally was able to go back to their living area Helen was with him.

"Pa said he had a surprise for me," she exclaimed, bursting into the room ahead of her father. "But he wouldn't tell me what it was." At that instant she saw John and stopped suddenly. Her cheeks crimsoned, making the freckles stand out even bolder than before. "John!" Her voice was almost a whisper.

She sat down across from him, eyeing him as though she could not believe he had actually returned. She was even more beautiful than he remembered. Her soft auburn hair fell around the delicate oval of her cheeks, hiding her ears. Her eyes were as blue as the deepest sky and her nose and cheekbones were still covered with freckles. He wondered if she hated them as much now as she had professed the last time he saw her.

"I'm so glad you came." Her smile said more than her words.

"What brings you back here after so long?" Matt asked.

John glanced at Helen and grinned. "Helen and I were reading a book we didn't get finished."

The color rushed back to her cheeks. "You're funnin' me," she said, suddenly shy and embarrassed.

"You'll never know how many times I've thought about that book and the very sweet young lady who was reading it to me to help pass those lonely hours."

She looked away quickly. In that instant John read something in her features that warmed his heart. She still thought about him. Maybe—just maybe—she thought about him the way he thought about her.

After a time Rebecca went to the kitchen to start supper, and Matt had an errand that took him across town.

"Why don't you two go into the parlor and get acquainted again?" Helen's mother suggested.

"I–I should help with supper," the girl said.

"Go along with you. There'll be time enough for that later."

He followed her into the parlor that was seldom used except on such occasions and sat in a platform rocker in the far corner. She took a chair across from him.

"I'm so glad you came back," she told him.

"I wanted to come a long time ago, but things didn't work out."

As they talked it seemed to John that he had never been away. She was the same sweet, bubbling girl she had been when he rode off two years before. And Matt and Rebecca were as friendly as ever.

"Do you notice anything that's missing?" Helen asked.

His forehead crinkled. "Everything seems the same to me."

"There's something that isn't here any more."

"You'll have to tell me."

"Elizabeth," the girl exclaimed. Her eyes danced. "She ran away and married Charlie Sims."

"I'm glad it wasn't you."

Her cheeks flushed. "Why would I want to run away and marry Charlie Sims?"

"I'm glad you didn't run away and marry anybody."

An embarrassed silence gripped them.

When Matt Norvall returned an hour later John and Helen were still in the parlor.

"Just had a funny thing happen, Helen," her father said, hanging his hat on the rack. "You know that gambler who checked in last week? I told you he was taking over the faro table at the Crystal Palace."

"Mr. Applegate?"

"That's right. Phineas Applegate. He closed his table and is heading west on the first stage. I thought he liked it here. At least that's what he told me," Matt continued, "but Cy Perkins said Applegate had a run-in with a stranger this afternoon. A big feller carrying a gun. It wasn't five minutes after the stranger left the Crystal Palace that the faro dealer packed up his gear and quit."

Helen surveyed Breckenridge quietly. His cheeks flushed as he realized that she was aware of the identity of the man her father was talking about. She said nothing, however, until her father went in to wash for supper.

"What was that about, John?" she asked. "The run-in you had with Mr. Applegate."

For some reason having her question him put

him on the defensive—as though he had to vindi-cate his actions. "Your Mr. Applegate had a horse that belonged to me. I went to get it back."

Helen had been vivacious and happy to that point. Now, however, she fell silent. A cloud seemed to mar her finely chiseled features.

"What's the matter?" he asked.

"Nothing."

"Is it about Rafferty?" he persisted. "Are you upset because he's leaving Ogallala?"

She shook her head.

"I–I was just hoping you'd changed. That's all."

"I couldn't let him get away with a good horse, could I?"

"We have a sheriff here. Or didn't you know?"

"The sheriff wouldn't have done me a bit of good. It would have been my word against the gambler's. With him known in town I wouldn't have had a chance."

She was silent for at least a minute. "So," she continued at last, "you made him give you the horse."

His features darkened. "I didn't have to do much making. Rafferty knew what he'd done and he knew that horse was mine. I'm not on the wrong side of the law, and that's the pure truth."

"You're on the wrong side of the law if you take things into your own hands," she informed him coldly.

His temper flamed. He didn't know why it was so tough trying to explain things to a woman!

17

The Norvall family and John Breckenridge were at
supper when the night clerk called Matt to the
desk.

"What was that all about?" Rebecca asked
when he returned.

"Applegate checked out and left a box of his
things at the hotel. He'll be sending for them
later, when he has a permanent address."

"I don't approve of the way he earns his living," Rebecca Norvall said, "but he does seem
like a nice man. And so neat and tidy."

John squirmed uncomfortably. He had the
feeling they were blaming him for the gambler's
sudden decision to leave.

"I can't imagine what could be in that box that
would be so important to Applegate," Matt continued. "He gave me twenty dollars to pay for
keeping it and sending it on to him."

"I can tell you," John blurted. He hadn't intended to speak, but he opened his mouth and the
words came out unbidden.

"How would you know?" Helen demanded,
suddenly defensive for their former guest. "You
haven't even seen it."

"I traveled with him. Remember?"

"If you're so sure of what's in the box," Helen said, "what is it?"

He wished he had kept quiet, but he hadn't. Now he had to continue. "He's a gambler and not too honest, so he'll have a special faro-dealing box with a few peculiar features to give him an edge when he needs it. He's also got some other items from the mail order house of Will & Finck, like misspotted dice, marked cards, shaved decks, and that sort of thing."

Helen's eyes widened. "Are they used for what I think they are?"

"If you want the blunt truth, they're the stock in trade of the crooked gambler. There are those who aren't satisfied to have the advantage of their skill over their opponents."

"A nice man like Mr. Applegate wouldn't cheat."

"A nice man wouldn't cheat," Breckenridge countered irritably. "I agree with you."

"I take it you don't like him much."

"That's right."

Rebecca was disturbed by the trend of the conversation. "I'm sure we can think of something else to talk about."

But her daughter was not going to be stopped. "Is that box of Mr. Applegate's wrapped and tied, Pa?"

"I couldn't say. I never looked at it."

"Well, I'd like to. I want to find out if he's everything John says he is."

"We can't rummage through his things," Rebecca protested.

Matt held out a coffee cup for his wife to refill it. "I've been thinking about what John said. I'm going to have to examine that box. If I'm supposed to mail it I have the right to know what I'm sending."

As soon as they finished supper they went up the back stairs to the gambler's room. Matt, who led them, struck a match and lit the kerosene lamp that was sitting on one corner of the buffet. The faint yellow glow revealed the washstand with a mirror over it and an iron bedstead with a sagging mattress. Along the opposite wall stood a chest of drawers. The box was on the floor at one end of the chest.

Norvall picked up the box that belonged to the gambler, set it on the bed, and raised the lid. There were two clean shirts neatly folded on top with a clean pair of pants underneath. Below the pants were several handkerchiefs and two black string ties.

"It's just clothes!" Helen exclaimed, a note of triumph creeping into her voice.

"We aren't through yet." Her father put the clothes on the bed and pulled a strange-looking object from the box.

"What's that?" she asked.

"That," John informed her, "is a device for storing and retrieving needed cards. With that contraption a gambler doesn't take any chances. He can know what cards he's dealing everyone in the game."

She turned to her father. "Is that right, Pa?"

He nodded silently.

The next was a card holdout device to be worn underneath cuffs, sleeves, or vests.

"Another very valuable item," Breckenridge informed her. "So is the smaller twenty-eight-number roulette wheel that gives the house gambler a thirteen percent advantage over his opponents. Then there's the faro casekeeper and the shear card trimmer. I don't know about you, Matt, but I'd say your Mr. Applegate and my Sam Rafferty was quite well prepared."

"It's a wonder he's been able to keep alive running a table with these things."

"He carries a derringer up his left sleeve. And he's had to shoot his way out more than once that I've heard about."

They were about to leave the room when Rebecca saw the sleeve of an old shirt sticking out from under the bed.

"What's this?" she asked, stooping.

"Looks like he forgot something," Breckenridge put in.

The shirt was wrapped about a big book.

"That's strange," Rebecca muttered, picking it up. "A Bible!"

John stared at it. "That was Elihu's!"

The hotel owner's wife opened the book and looked at the flyleaf. "How did you know?"

"I ought to. I got it out of Wiggin's gear after he was shot and killed. The last I saw it was in my saddlebags. Rafferty must've taken it before he ran out on us."

Helen took the Bible from her mother and leafed through it hurriedly. "If Mr. Applegate was the kind of man you said he was," she asked, "why would he carry a Bible with him? There had to be something there."

Breckenridge shrugged. "Who knows why a character like Rafferty would do anything? I've known men who had a Bible for a good luck charm."

When Helen finished looking at it, her father

gave it to John. "Applegate was going to throw it away. If you want it, take it."

They went back to the parlor and sat down. Matt started to settle in for the evening, but Rebecca got him into the kitchen. "Helen and John have a lot to talk about," she told him.

When they were again alone they eyed each other uncomfortably.

"I reckon I owe you an apology," Helen said, "You were right about Mr. Applegate. He was so polite and thoughtful, I couldn't believe he would do anything that wasn't honest."

"There are lots of guys like that," he told her. "But it's like my step-pa used to say, 'you can't judge a book by its cover.'"

They remained in the parlor until the clock struck ten. Breckenridge knew the time had come to go up to his room.

"You aren't leaving right away, are you?" she asked, her usually happy features suddenly serious.

"Not for a few days."

"I wish you could stay."

Momentarily he stared beyond her at the heavy drapery that covered the double windows. There was no reason why he couldn't stay in the little Nebraska town as long as he wanted to. He could come and go as he pleased.

But John was a driven man. He had to have revenge for what Kramer and the others had done. He would not be content until he had. He would stay in Ogallala a few days and then go on, searching for the cattle thief until he found him. Only he didn't say anything to Helen about that. He knew how hurt she would be.

Yet it was not easy for him to go. Four days passed and a week. He and Helen went for rides along the Platte and in the hills north of town. They had picnics in the shade of a clump of cottonwoods, and he taught her to shoot his rifle.

He didn't know how Harry Kessler learned about his riding or thought there was a chance of hiring him to break a new string of saddle broncs. But the rancher showed up at the hotel one morning with an offer of several months' work.

"I've got some wild stock we rounded up and some colts I've raised that need to be broken to ride. I hear tell you can handle the bad ones."

"I get thrown once in awhile, but I've been riding since I was a kid."

"That's what I figured. You want the job?"

Breaking broncs was no job to stay with very long, but it would give Breckenridge some money and an excuse to hang around Ogallala. "I'll come for a spell," he replied.

He told Helen about his new job and her eyes brightened. "Pa and Ma will be pleased about that."

"I was in hopes that you would want me to stay, too."

Her smile winked at him.

John started breaking horses for the Slash-J Bar and kept at it for a number of weeks until the trees turned color and the buffalo grass began to brown. He thought he was finished on several occasions, but the rancher continued to find horses for him to break. He green-broke those that were to be sold but spent more time on those for the remuda. The best three of the lot were to be well broken and gentled for the rancher's wife and two daughters.

Twice a week John rode into town to see Helen. Theirs was a comfortable relationship. They seldom argued, except at first when she tried to convince him he shouldn't bear any ill feelings towards the man who was responsible for the death of his friends and the loss of cattle. After that he kept quiet about the rage that burned within him and things went better.

Having a place of his own began to interest him as he and Helen spent more time together. It would be good to own a spread, he decided. Then they could settle down together and have a couple of boys—and a girl who looked just like Helen. And at night, after the work was done, they would be able to sit in front of the house, looking out over their land and their cattle, with kids playing at their feet.

He didn't remember when he and Helen first started talking about marriage and getting that place of their own. It hadn't been too long after he started breaking horses for the Slash-J Bar.

Matt wasn't too surprised when John went to him about it. "I'd be right proud to have you in the family. I can use a good man in the hotel."

Breckenridge tugged at the lobe of his ear. "I don't reckon I'm cut out for the hotel business."

"I didn't figure you were, but it didn't hurt to try. You've got a head on your shoulders."

Helen and Rebecca began to prepare for the wedding. They sent to Kansas City for material for a dress and wrote to the itinerate preacher in North Platte about coming up to marry them.

Helen had always been a vivacious, loving child, but she was happier than her parents had ever seen her. Yet when Rebecca went to Helen's room one evening a few days before the wedding, she was sprawled across the bed, tears scalding her cheeks.

"Don't let it bother you, Helen," she said, sitting on the bed and putting an arm about her. "Most girls get the jitters before they're married. I did. I wondered if I loved Matt and if he loved me, but everything turned out wonderful for us."

Helen dabbed at the tears with a corner of her handkerchief. "That's not it, Ma."

"We know John's not going to be content breaking horses for the Slash-J Bar, and he's not the kind to come into the hotel. He's a cattle-man."

Helen was silent for a time before continuing. "It's not that, either. We've talked it over. I'm going to have to leave Ogallala. He wants to drive cattle until he gets money enough to get a small spread somewhere." She paused and wiped at her eyes once more.

"What is it, then?"

"It's the gun he wears and the look he gets when he talks about that man Kramer. He carries an awful hatred, Ma. He's a different person when he talks about him. I–I'm almost afraid of him."

Rebecca breathed deeply. "If it's that seri-ous—and I guess I'd feel the same way—you'd better get things sorted out in your own mind before you get married."

The tears flowed again.

"Maybe you ought to give back his ring."

"But I love him so much! I–I don't even want to live without him." She looked up at her mother helplessly. "Oh, Ma! What shall I do?"

Tears mingled on their cheeks, and for the space of several minutes they clung to each other.

Rebecca talked with Matt that night and they both discussed the matter with their daughter in the morning, but she had already settled her mind. She loved John and was going to marry him.

The wedding took place as planned. Rev. Marcus Thornbloom performed the ceremony, which was held in the hotel. Helen was well liked in the community, and the hotel lobby was packed for the ceremony. She was strangely quiet that morning, but Breckenridge was so nervous he didn't even notice.

They stayed around Ogallala until the first of the week. John collected his wages from the ranch, and they started for Texas where he planned to make arrangements with a number of small spreads to take cattle north for them. He would take his pay in stock and when he got enough to make such a venture profitable he would find a place in Wyoming or Montana and they would settle down.

Saying good-bye was tearful. John stood uncomfortably to one side, while Helen and Rebecca clung to each other.

"Makes me feel like I've done something wrong, taking Helen away from her ma," Breckenridge said to Matt.

"It ain't that. Becky wants Helen to go with you."

"She's got a funny way of showing it."

Norvall's smile was empty, but it served to hide the pain he was experiencing. "Wait until you have a daughter who gets married and moves a long ways away. Then you'll understand."

Helen was still crying as they got on the Denver-bound train. John leaned back in the seat and closed his eyes. For a time the tears continued coursing down his young wife's cheeks. Finally she dabbed at them with the corner of her handkerchief and looked up at him.

"I'm sorry, John," she said softly.

"Feel better?"

"I will."

They were in Denver several days before catching the southbound stage. It was Helen's first visit to a city larger than North Platte and her first view of the mountains. She was fascinated by both.

"I don't ever want to leave," she told him.

"I felt the same way the first time I was here. Wait till you get up on top of some of those peaks. You'd swear you could see forever."

They jounced out of Denver early in the morning on the southbound stage. It was slow, uncomfortable going, and John glanced at Helen occasionally to see how she was doing.

The stage was full out of Denver, but at the first stop most of the passengers got off. Two well-dressed business men from Chicago joined Breckenridge and his wife and the wife and daughter of a Cottonwood Springs banker.

They hadn't been on their way long when John scrunched in the corner and closed his eyes, trying to sleep. Helen folded her hands in her lap, bouncing and swaying with the lurch of the cumbersome stage. The seven-year-old girl squirmed uncomfortably and chattered to Helen, who was sitting next to her.

"My pa is going to be surprised," she said. "We left Grandma's place in St. Louis a week early and came out as far as we could by train. Now we're almost home and he's going to be so surprised! I can hardly wait."

"Eloise," her mother ordered, exhaustion stealing the strength from her voice, "don't talk all the time. The lady is tired of listening to you."

The bright-eyed girl turned thoughtfully to Helen. "You aren't tired of talking to me, are you?" There was a certain pleading tone in her voice.

"Of course not. I think talking helps make the time go by faster."

"So do I." She looked up at her mother. "It's all right if I talk to Mrs. Breckenridge, isn't it, Ma?"

The older woman sighed wearily. "If she doesn't mind I don't suppose I should."

One of the men from Chicago took a fat cigar from his vest pocket, turned it momentarily between his fingers, as though trying to decide whether to light it or not. He must have changed his mind. He returned the cigar to his pocket, brushed the dust off his expensive coat, and glanced out the window.

"'Pears as though we're about to have company," he said, a strange apprehension creeping into his voice. "There's four riders headed this way!"

18

Breckenridge, who had been almost asleep, sat up quickly and looked out. The riders were racing towards them at top speed! By this time the driver and "shotgun" rider had seen the men and reached the same conclusion. John snatched up his rifle, opened the door, and climbed up on top, while Helen watched in growing terror.

"Need help?" he shouted.

"Looks like we're going to need every gun we can get."

"There won't be anything from below," Breckenridge informed the guard riding shotgun. "Them two from Chicago are scared to death!"

They waited tensely until the hard-riding quartet of outlaws were within range. John, who had his rifle at his shoulder, squeezed the trigger. The big gun roared and the nearest bandit plunged off his powerful mount to the hard prairie sod. Another mount stumbled and almost went down. The guard riding shotgun squeezed off a shot, hitting the tawny-haired brigand in the stomach. The force of the slug doubled him up, and his horse veered away. Somehow the highwayman got a handful of mane and clung to the back of his hard-running animal, but not for long. His strength ebbed and he fell to the ground.

The driver shouted a warning, and John swung to the opposite side, firing rapidly as three more of the gang galloped in from an arroyo that opened almost on the trail's edge. The nearest of the trio screamed in pain and frustration as a bullet slammed into him.

The stage driver took a slug in the shoulder and shouted for help with the reins as he slumped in the seat. John scrambled forward, pushed the injured man to one side and jerked the leather straps from his tightly clenched fingers. His voice raised above the din as he urged the six-horse team to even greater speed. The valiant animals strained in the harness, jerking the stagecoach wildly over the rutted trail.

After the furious exchange, the highwaymen had had enough. They turned and dashed for the hills. Still, Breckenridge did not slacken speed. He kept the powerful horses running hard until he was certain the holdup gang had actually given up. Then he eased off and the team slowed.

Not until then did he realize that the guard on top with him had been wounded. The bluff, gray-haired marksman who had been guarding stages longer than anyone could remember groaned feebly. John managed a quick glance over his shoulder. The old man swayed and the rifle he used so effectively slipped from his grasp. By this time the lathered horses had come to a stop. They stood motionless, trembling from exertion, their heavy breathing torn from aching lungs.

Breckenridge tied the reins deftly over the post at his right hand and went back to check the rifleman. The wounded man was holding his stomach with both hands, desperately trying to stanch the flow of blood.

"We did it!" he managed between clenched teeth.

By this time the passengers had opened the stagecoach door and were getting out, visibly shaken. Eloise Harmon was crying and the men from Chicago were pale and quavering.

"Give me a hand!" John ordered. "We've got to get these men down."

The travelers reached up and took the injured rifleman from Breckenridge and laid him on the grass. His face was gray and torn with pain.

Helen knelt beside the more severely wounded patient. Tearing the bottom from her petticoat, she stuffed as much cloth as she could in the hole to stop the bleeding. The other woman joined her but, even as she did so, they realized their efforts were useless. The injured man opened his eyes and tried to talk, but he could not. His body shuddered and his head went limp.

"He's gone!" the older woman gasped.

John wrapped the body in a blanket and with the help of one of the male passengers, boosted it up on top and tied it in place. Helen's eyes filled with tears, but she dared not cry. Even though one patient had died, there was still work to do. While Breckenridge was taking care of the body, the two women directed their attention to the wounded driver. They stopped the flow of blood from his arm with a crude tourniquet and cleaned out the wound. One of the male passengers brought out a bottle of whiskey and they poured it in and around the bullet hole as a disinfectant. Then they wrapped the wound securely.

"Help me back on top," he protested. "I've got to get this stage into Cottonwood Springs."

"You'll do nothing of the kind. My husband will take care of that."

"It's my job!" he exclaimed again.

"Not today," Breckenridge said firmly. He ordered the driver into the coach, and the man did as he was told. He turned to Helen who was on one side helping him. "You're a right purty gal," he said, winking at her. "I think I'll enjoy this ride."

She scarcely heard him. Her very being quivered and her heart beat fiercely against her chest. For a moment she thought she was going to be sick. She left the others and stood alone, staring helplessly into the distance. Breckenridge finished the grisly task and joined her.

"Are you all right?"

"Why did it have to happen? And to such a nice man?"

"You'll have to ask those thieving bandits."

"What if we'd stopped when they came riding up and had given them our money?" she asked numbly. "Was it worth that man's life?"

He was slow in answering her, and she repeated the question.

"I suppose it depends on how you look at it." John breathed deeply. "They might have killed us all."

"Do you really think so?"

"Money wouldn't have satisfied them when they saw you and the other lady! They'd have wanted the two of you and nothing short of shooting would have stopped them."

Anger twisted his rugged features. "But that's only part of the story. How can we ever build a safe country with homes and churches and stores if the decent people don't rid the place of such scum? Honorable men, like our friend whose body is on top of the stage, have to stand up to that kind or there'll be no place anyone will be safe." His eyes pleaded desperately for understanding. "I know you don't like this gun I carry, but someone's got to stand up to that kind of trash and say, 'You've gone far enough! We aren't putting up with your kind any more.'"

Before she could answer, one of the men from Chicago approached. "Can we go now?" he asked. "Maybe hoodlums will try again!"

John touched his wife on the arm. "Are you sure you're all right?"

"I'm fine." She smiled weakly up at him.

They were only twelve miles from Cottonwood Springs, the place where they were to spend the night. The team, rested somewhat from the furious pace he drove them during the chase, was eager to be off. He took them into town at a brisk pace. The big vehicle careened around the corner and charged up the street, past the livery barn and two general stores, to stop in front of the hotel. As usual there was a double handful of men and women waiting to meet the stage. One of the regulars noticed that Jedediah Smith, who had been riding shotgun and the driver, Tommy Abrams, were not in their rightful places. Those who were knowledgeable saw the blanket-wrapped body and guessed what had happened.

"Where's Jedediah and Tommy?" a pudgy storekeeper demanded.

"Bandits tried to stop us," Eloise Harmon said excitedly when none of the adults replied to the question. "But Mr. Breckenridge chased them away."

"I knew it!" someone else cried. "Now that we've got no marshal the outlaws are taking advantage of us!"

The story that the stage had been robbed spread rapidly. It wasn't long until everyone in town knew that the Wimberly stage had been held up, the driver wounded, and Jedediah Smith killed. The burly passengers from Chicago related what had happened in elaborate detail that increased with each telling.

"If it hadn't been for him," one of them said, "we'd all have been killed."

Craig Harmon, whose wife and small daughter had been on the stage, turned to his wife. "Is that true?"

"When those outlaws attacked, Mr. Breckenridge went up on top and rode shotgun with Jedediah. He helped drive those awful men away. And when Tommy was wounded he took over the driving." She paused thoughtfully. "He saved us all."

Harmon's face was pale and drawn and his hands shook. He took John's hand impulsively. "I don't know how I can ever thank you."

Breckenridge waved him aside with a quick, embarrassed gesture. "We were after saving our own necks, too."

"Just the same, I'm beholden to you. Where are you staying the night?" he asked.

"We'll be at the hotel."

John excused himself as quickly as he could and went into the frontier hotel with Helen. It was built of the same cheap lumber and had the same worn look as the rest of the town, though it was comparatively new. It was bigger than the hotel Helen's parents operated, but it had the same captain's chairs and small writing tables. A dining room opened off to one side, and across the lobby a door led to a small but dignified saloon. It was the sort of place where men with money and an urge to drink or gamble would feel comfortable, knowing they were associating with their peers.

They followed the clerk to their room on the second floor, washed up and changed into clean clothes. When they went down to the dining room an hour later, Harmon, his wife, and two other couples were waiting for them.

The banker introduced John and Helen to his associates. "This is Adolph and Francine Kellerman. They have the general store here—the big one next to the bank." He indicated the slender, graying storekeeper and his kindly, well-upholstered wife. "And this is Emil Parker and his wife, Wilma. Emil is the Wells Fargo man here in Cottonwood."

Breckenridge eyed the trio of businessmen curiously as Harmon suggested they go in and sit down. Evidently there was more to the meeting than hospitality or even gratitude.

Finally Harmon turned to John. "I'm sure you're wondering what this is all about."

"The thought had crossed my mind," he replied evenly.

"Our marshal got killed a few weeks ago. We've been looking for someone to fill his place, but we haven't been able to find anybody." He paused and glanced at his companions.

"After what you did this afternoon I feel that you're the man for us," the banker added.

"You've proved yourself. I told Adolph and Emil that you're exactly what we need—"

"And we both agree," the Wells Fargo agent broke in. "Would you be interested in staying here as our marshal?"

"We had a meeting of the town council a few minutes ago. You're our choice."

"We hadn't planned on taking a job," John said lamely. "We're on our way to Texas."

"Have you got family down there?" the banker persisted. "Do you have a ranch or a business waiting for you?"

"Nope," Breckenridge said. "Nothing like that."

"Then there's no reason why you can't stay on here and help us. At least for awhile—until we find someone else to take your place."

He told them he wasn't interested and thought that would end the matter, but they were insistent.

"We'll furnish you a place to live and pay you one hundred dollars a month for as long as you want to stay."

John's eyes widened. "I've never earned as much as one hundred dollars a month on a job in my whole life!" he exclaimed.

Their food came and they started to eat. When they finished and were dawdling over their after-supper coffee Harmon directed his attention to Helen.

"I'm sure you would find Cottonwood a charming place. We have a school with a good teacher and a church. I understand there's going to be a parson moving in the first of the month." He turned to his wife. "Isn't that right, dear?"

"That's when we're expecting him."

Harmon glanced at Helen. "The way I figure it, a little religion never hurt anyone."

"What Harmon's trying to say," Parker put in, "is that Cottonwood Springs is a nice place for a young couple to settle down and raise a family."

"You'll have your work cut out for you, at least for awhile," Adolph Kellerman added. "There's a rough element here who'd like to take over if they could. That's why we need someone with a cool head and a quick draw. Someone like you. But once you get control, they'll move on and there won't be any problem in keeping the peace."

Breckenridge was slow in answering. He sipped his coffee and studied the faces of the men at the table. "Helen and I'll talk it over. We'll let you know in the morning."

"Sounds good," Harmon said, managing a thin, patronizing smile.

They got to their feet.

"We'll have breakfast with you tomorrow."

John and Helen went back to their room.

"Well," he said, once the door closed behind them. "What do you think?"

"I could like it here." Her smile faded and her eyes narrowed fearfully. "Only I don't know how it would be having you on the streets all the time with your gun and being responsible for all the trouble that comes along." She got to her feet and put her arms around him. "I couldn't stand it if anything happened to you."

He lifted her chin to look into her eyes. "Forget that sort of talk. Nothing is going to happen to me." Keeping his arm about her he guided her to the window where they looked out on the darkened street. "It would be a nice place for you to live," he continued. "And a good place to wait for Kramer!"

Her slender young frame tightened. "Is that all you can think of?"

"I've been wondering how I was going to be able to find him. I promised I wouldn't drag you all over the country looking for him."

"I thought we settled that. You weren't going to hunt for him any more."

He smiled bleakly, and the chill of it deadened the joy that had been hers since they were married.

"You promised, John."

"That's just it. If we stay here, the chances are I won't have to look for him. Cottonwood Springs is on the most traveled trail from Montana to Texas. Sooner or later Kramer will come this way."

"And if he doesn't?"

"I gave you my word. I won't go after him."

"Then you're going to take the job?" she asked.

"I was figuring on it, if it's all right with you."

19

Harmon and his friends were pleased when John told them that he would take the job.

As soon as they finished breakfast, Helen excused herself and went back to their room while John went with the town councilmen to the marshal's office where he was sworn in. There were certain laws they were anxious to see enforced, they said, but they weren't going to tell him how to run the office. He was the marshal. He had their authorization to do whatever seemed best.

When he was alone half an hour or so later he went behind the desk and sat down, looking things over in his new office. The handcuffs and keys were in a top drawer on top of a copy of the town's ordinances and regulations that he would be enforcing.

The bottom drawer at his left contained two coffee cups, a paper sack of Arbuckle's Coffee, and some sugar the mice had been in. He poured the sugar in the stove and cleaned out the mouse droppings and the beginning of a nest where the little creatures were planning on setting up housekeeping.

Breckenridge continued to go through the drawers, mechanically checking the contents of each. In the right-hand bottom drawer he exposed a pile of yellowed "wanted" posters. He thumbed through them, and the smudge marks he saw revealed that he wasn't the first to do so. He recognized some that he knew were already dead—desperados who had been killed in saloon fights or attempted robberies. Others he recognized by name—bad men still roaming the outlaw trail, trying to keep the law of might in force. They couldn't read the change that was coming to the West and used their six-guns and rifles to get what they wanted. Breckenridge had never heard of some other names. Most were young and smooth-cheeked, determined to make a name for themselves. And unfortunately for them, all too many died at it.

He continued to examine the posters curiously. If Kramer and Murray and Gilson were still alive, he might find new posters on them. Few were able to live as they did without getting on somebody's "wanted" list. He opened the other drawers in turn, but apparantly the former marshal had kept all of the posters in one place.

He returned the posters to the desk and closed the drawer. Then, deliberately, he got to his feet, pulled on his wool mackinaw, and stepped out into the harsh north wind. A tumbleweed came bouncing down the all-but-empty street, and a saddle horse, tied to the rail in front of Kellerman's General Store, shied at it, almost breaking free.

It was still early in the fall and the leaves had not yet fallen, but the chill of approaching winter was in the air. Cottonwood Springs was on the eastern edge of the foothills and the Rockies were visible in the distance, the jagged mountain ridge standing ugly and forbidding against the slate gray of the sky. Although the town was on the prairie the elevation was high enough to bring fall to the area long before it reached the plains. In a few short weeks ice would be blanketing the creeks and ponds, and the hay for the livestock would be stacked close to the ranch buildings.

It was John's first trip up the town's only business street as marshal. His every move would be watched for some sign that would indicate what he was made of. He maintained a leisurely pace down the boardwalk, pausing at store windows and looking in on the blacksmith and the gun shop. Men shook hands with him and welcomed him to Cottonwood.

He went into the saloon nearest the marshal's office and informed the bartender that the town council wanted the new gun law strictly enforced.

"Sounds all right to me," the barkeeper said, wiping his hands on the corner of his dirty apron. "When they come in, I'll tell them. But you'd just as well know it, Marshal. I'm not going to stick my neck out making them do it. That's what you're paid for."

"Fair enough."

The morning passed rapidly and by the time he reached the Lucky Dollar Saloon a number of hands from a nearby ranch had ridden in to uncork the boredom that had gripped them from a month in the hills riding herd. They came with money in their pockets and looking for trouble. Three were at the roulette wheel; another was sitting at a small table with a saloon girl. Several more were at the bar, drunk and belligerent.

"Look who's here!" Moses Shelley, the biggest of the lot, blustered. "Ain't that nice?

They've got themselves a real, live lawman. They want to keep things nice and peaceful as a cemetery."

John's pale eyes met Shelley's and held there. "That's the idea," he said. "We want the town to be nice and peaceful." He looked from one cowboy to another. It was obvious that the men came mostly from the same ranch.

"I hear tell they've got a new gun law. Right, Marshal?" Contempt edged Shelley's voice.

"You know just about everything, don't you?" Breckenridge said, keeping his voice mild and somewhat friendly. "Saves me the trouble of spreading the word." He paused. "So if you boys'll just take off your guns and bring them over to the bartender, he'll keep 'em until you've had your fun and are ready to go back to the ranch."

The big cowhand pushed forward, his whiskered features twisted contemptuously. "And if we don't?"

John smiled coldly and his voice did not falter. "I reckon I'll have to take them away from you." He paused.

"Is that a fact?" the cowboy bellowed. His laughter rang through the long building. "We'll have to see about that!"

By this time all activity in the saloon had ceased. The cowhands were watching their hero expectantly, knowing his strength and his quickness with the gun slung low on his hip. His legs were spread slightly and his hand hovered over the butt of his iron. Those who might have been in the line of fire, edged to either side.

"You'd better go on about your business, Marshal. We'll just forget you ever came in here and started ordering us around."

179

"You'd better do what he says, sonny," an older hand put in. "It'd be a shame to have to leave off our drinking to haul you to the undertakin' parlor. It'd plumb spoil our day."

One of the roulette players snickered.

John studied the situation carefully. It could explode into violence. But he dare not back down. Word would spread and there wouldn't be a roughneck in the area who would pay attention to anything he said.

"I'll start with you," Breckenridge said to Moses Shelley, who was grinning drunkenly. "Take off your gun belt and put it on the bar."

For answer the cowhand spit a stream of tobacco juice into John's face. The law officer's temper exploded. His powerful right snaked out with lightning speed. He grabbed the big man by the shirt collar, jerking him forward. Just as swiftly he released his hold and swung his left, his open hand catching the drunken cowboy on the cheek. The blow knocked him into a chair. He fell, overturning a table and crashing heavily to the floor. Cursing violently, he scrambled to his knees and clawed for his weapon, but not in time. He was staring helplessly into the barrel of John's hogleg.

"I'll kill you!"

"Spit tobacco juice in my face again and you'll have your chance! Now get up and take that gun belt off!"

He didn't move.

"You heard me! Take it off!"

"And if I don't?" he blustered, the words dribbling between thick lips.

"I'll take it myself!" Holding the Colt .44 on the man he had knocked to the floor, he loosed the gun belt and jerked it free. "The rest of the boys'll get their guns back when they leave town today, but not you! You'll get yours when I get ready to give it to you."

"When's that going to be?" Moses Shelley demanded. By this time the fight was all but out of him.

"It might be a week. It might be a month. It depends on how.well you behave yourself."

He got uncertainly to his feet and remained motionless, leaning on the table for support. A weak grin twisted his features. Breckenridge deliberately turned from him and surveyed the stunned hands who had ridden to town with Shelley. "Anybody else who's got any ideas about keeping his gun?" He stared from one to the other.

They went up to the bar, silently, and took off their belts.

"All right, barkeep," he directed. "Take care of them. And don't let anybody have his weapon back until he's had his belly full of drinking and is ready to leave town. Understand?"

He nodded crisply.

"If they give you any trouble, just send for me!"

"That I'll do." Respect replaced the doubt he had shown earlier. The marshal had passed the first test of will.

He picked up the weapon he had taken from the drunken cowhand and went through the swinging doors into the slate gray morning. He could still hear the man he had disarmed cursing violently and shouting threats to the wind. John stopped on the corner and mopped the sweat and the last traces of tobacco juice from his face.

181

Word of the showdown with the big cowhand spread rapidly throughout the little community. Moses Shelley was well known for his bullying. Even his own men steered clear of him when he was on a spree. And more than one silently cheered Breckenridge on for standing up to the boisterous, ugly-tempered giant of a man.

"That character had it coming," the blacksmith told him. "Everybody in town's been afraid to spit when he was on the prowl." He threw back his balding head and cackled. "I'd have given a 'purty' to have seen it!"

John did not tell Helen what had happened, but she soon heard about it. The waitress in the hotel dining room mentioned it first, and two of the ladies who came to pay their respects said they were so glad he had backed Shelley down without bloodshed.

That night, resting her head on his shoulder she asked about it. "Is that the way it's going to be?"

"The man was drunk."

"Will every drunk you meet try to goad you into a fight?"

He was silent, wanting to reassure her about his safety without lying. The truth was he didn't know what to expect. There would be a period of testing—a time when men would want to to see just how determined he was to keep the peace.

"I wish we had gone on to Texas," she said. "At least you wouldn't be facing this sort of thing."

Mrs. Harmon and Francine Kellerman came and got her the following afternoon and took her over to the house they were fixing up for her and John. They had hired someone to clean it, and they were re-papering the living room and washing the windows. Some of the furniture had already been brought in and the rest would be there by the end of the week.

The women stayed at it and by the end of the week the house was livable. John and Helen moved in. She was happier now that they were out of the hotel and had a place of their own. Ever since she could remember she had lived in a hotel. Now for the first time she had a place of her own. She was excited about arranging the furniture to suit herself and being able to prepare whatever she wanted to for meals.

That first Saturday she went to the Kellerman store for food, and when Breckenridge got home that evening she had supper ready. She had picked out the meat herself, as well as the potatoes and vegetables.

He pulled out a chair and sat down.

"Does everything look all right?" she asked nervously. It was the first meal she had prepared for him without having her mother in the kitchen with her.

When they finished eating they lingered at the table over coffee.

"Do you have to work tomorrow?" she asked hopefully.

"Not unless something comes up."

"I–I thought maybe you'd go to church with me tomorrow."

He was surprised at the question.

"I've been meaning to talk to you about it," she continued, "about going to church, I mean. But—"

"But, what?"

"I was afraid you wouldn't."

He thought for a moment. He hadn't been to church much, that was sure. The only time he could remember was when his ma died and they had her funeral in the little church at Weaverville. He didn't even know what they did in a regular meeting. But Helen wanted him to go. He wasn't keen on it but he guessed it couldn't hurt him much.

"When did you get started at that?"

"I've been going to tell you," she said. "Last spring a preacher came to town from somewhere and started holding meetings. He brought along an accordian player and his wife who sang. Almost everybody in town came to hear the music if nothing else."

She paused and he waited for her to continue.

"That was the reason Ma and I went—at least at first—but then we started listening to the things the preacher was saying. He started asking questions."

"Like what?" Breckenridge cut in quickly. "What kind of questions?"

"Questions like, 'Where are you going to go when you die?'"

"I know where you'd go!" he told her. "A finer woman than you has never lived! You won't have to worry about that!"

"I won't now," she exclaimed, her face shining. "I'm a Christian! I've confessed my sin and put my trust in Jesus Christ to save me."

He stared at her incredulously. "I don't get it."

Helen tried to explain so he could understand but wasn't able to do so. "Maybe when you start going to church you will."

John went in to the bedroom and returned

with Elihu's Bible. "You'd just as well have this," he said, dropping it on her lap.

"But it belonged to your friend," she protested.

"You'll use it," he muttered gruffly. "That's what it's for."

Hearing the preacher might make him understand about Helen and this new faith, or whatever you wanted to call it, that made her so happy. But he wouldn't count on it.

The following morning he got ready when Helen did and they walked to the meeting place together. The new parson wasn't there yet, but a rancher's son took care of the speaking. He read from the Bible about forgiveness and how each person had to confess his sin and put his trust in Jesus Christ if he was to be pardoned so he could go to heaven.

John wasn't quite ready to accept those things for his own life, but he had to admit that he been had powerfully interested in what Helen and the youthful speaker had to say. After the service, however, he said as little as possible to his wife about the sermon.

20

Fall gave way to winter in the high plains and snow swept down from the Rockies, blanketing the prairies and taking its toll of livestock and game. The mercury plummeted to the bottom of the tube and hung there, while storm after storm buffeted the area.

Breckenridge continued to make his rounds of the saloons and eating places and stores along the main street. The town was comparatively quiet during that period—not that he didn't have problems. Twice, shortly after the affair with Shelley, young toughs got liquored up and decided to find out for themselves what the new marshal was made of.

They soon found out. The first picked a quarrel over leaving his gun at the bar and started to draw. John slammed him against the wall so hard his weapon flew halfway across the room, and his head still throbbed the next day when the marshal let him out of jail.

The next time in town his friend, a burly young hoodlum almost as big as Moses Shelley, claimed John called him a liar and started for him. Breckenridge moved nimbly to one side and slammed his powerful left into the cowhand's belly. The right that followed knocked the would-be brawler across a table into the bar. It took two of his friends to carry him to the jail, and it was half an hour before he regained consciousness.

Those incidents were as widely known as John's run-in with Moses Shelley. After that he had no more difficulties. The job became almost boring.

Christmas came, and with it the worst snow of the season. It swooped out of the mountains and raged across the plains, blocking roads and locking people in their homes. Cattle and horses died of the cold and starvation, and so did men if they were unfortunate enough to be caught out in it. For five days John wasn't able to leave the house. Nothing uptown was open—not even the saloons that boasted of never closing.

People were beginning to run out of supplies and coal before the wind and snow relented and began to ease their viselike grip on the prairies. The first day after the storm stopped and the men scooped out Cottonwood Springs, the town was crowded.

"I've never seen anything like it," John said wearily, sitting in the back porch and pulling off his boots, "It's like two Saturdays, Christmas, and the Fourth of July all rolled into one."

"Will the stage be through?" his wife asked.

"They're beginning to get the snow moved in town, but my guess is the road to Corning Bluffs and Wimberly is still blocked."

The next morning the sun broke through the even gray cloud cover. The day was bright with promise but cold as the snow that had preceded it. And the wind that whipped over the open land

187

was harsh and bitter. It was still no day to be out.

Yet John had to make his rounds. He was later than usual when he rode over the snow-covered road to the Lucky Dollar Saloon. There were only two horses tied in front and the building was quiet. John thought at first that he would go on without stopping. It was obvious that there were no problems at the Lucky Dollar that day. Yet there was a disturbing familiarity about the horses hunched at the hitching rail. He swung off the line-back dun and went inside.

The big, almost empty room was comparatively dark, and it took a moment for his eyes to adjust to the change of light. The bartender was draped over the polished mahogany, half asleep, and two men were sitting at a corner table facing the door.

Breckenridge started suddenly. Gilson and Murray! Cold rage seethed in his pale eyes and the muscles about his mouth tightened. He moved towards them in slow, catlike steps. By this time they recognized him as well. Their faces flushed and they scooted back from the table.

"If it ain't Breckenridge!" Gilson exclaimed, a smile gleaming from his evil, wrinkled features.

"And wearing a badge!" Bull Murray added. "Our old trail boss a lawman! You have come up in the world!"

"Sit down and have a beer!" Gilson raised his voice. "Barkeep! Bring us another beer for our friend."

"I don't want a beer," John snapped. "And I'm not your friend!" He paused briefly. "What're you doing here?"

"This's a free country," Murray exclaimed. "We can go where we please!"

"We didn't see any 'keep out' signs on the edge of town," Emil Gilson added.

"What're you doing in Cottonwood?" Breckenridge persisted.

"We just stopped by to see you. That's all right, ain't it?"

"We're willing to let bygones be bygones—if you are."

"You taught us a lesson," Gilson said. "We don't want to tangle with you again if we can help it."

"You were in on stealing my herd!"

"What herd?"

"The one you and Kramer and them other rustlers took from us!" John's eyes slitted and his anger flamed.

"We never had anything to do with taking your herd," Gilson told him. "And that's a fact."

Murray nodded vigorously. "I'm going to tell you what happened after we went to town that night. Kramer and Jake was roaring drunk and it didn't take us long to join 'em."

John waited without comment.

"Anyway, the sheriff throwed us in jail and kept us for a week."

"Go on."

"When we got out Kramer was all for a fight. He couldn't talk about anything but getting back at that gambler and you. Well, we didn't want any more trouble, so Bull and me took off. We went up into the mountains west of Denver and tried our luck at prospecting."

"We didn't do too bad, neither," Murray added. "Got us enough color to last through the winter and then some."

"The only problem was when we got back

down to Denver. We met Kramer at one of them saloons on Laramie Street and went on another rip-roarin' drunk."

"Whooee!" Bull Murray exclaimed. "My head still hurts just thinking about it!"

"When we finally sobered up we was in jail again. Didn't have no money and Kramer wasn't anywhere around." He placed both hands flat on the table and looked up into John's icy features. "That's the last we saw of him. He helped himself to our dust and took off."

Breckenridge didn't believe the story. "What're you doing here?" he repeated.

"We've been down on our luck lately. So we started looking for work. We were in a little town west of here—don't recollect the name right now. Anyway, we heard the Circle R over this way is looking for hands so we rode over to have us a look."

The corners of John's mouth tightened. "Most spreads in these parts don't put on new hands in the winter time."

Emil Gilson groaned. "That's about our luck."

"I run a tight town," John said. "See that you don't cause any trouble or you'll be in jail again."

"You won't have no problems with us. We've had our share of trouble."

John turned on his heel and left, pausing at the swinging doors and looking back. Murray waved to him.

Breckenridge expected Gilson and Murray to be in the Cottonwood area for several days. They would be completely sober, traveling from one spread to another even though it took weeks or months. Then they would come back into town,

190

lay one on, and stay drunk until most of their money was gone. When he returned to the Lucky Dollar the next morning, however, they were gone. He asked the bartender about them.

"All I know is that they didn't come in."

"Any idea where they went?"

The barkeeper shrugged. "They asked how much the hotel charges for rooms and how to get out to the Circle R. That's all I know."

John checked with the clerk at the hotel and found that Murray and Gilson had spent the night there, renting one room for both of them. And they left after breakfast.

"Acted like they were in a hurry," the clerk concluded. "They were talking about going to some ranch before all the jobs were taken. I tried to tell them nobody was hiring these days, but they wouldn't listen."

John went back to his office, built up the fire once more, and made a pot of coffee. He was pouring a cup for himself when the door opened and a familiar voice spoke. "Mornin', Marshal!"

John whirled, staring at the big man who almost filled the doorway. "Kramer!"

"Breckenridge! What're you doing here?"

21

"I heard you were dead!" Kramer ventured.

Fury laced John's voice. "You didn't do as good a job of shooting me in the back as you thought."

"Now, wait a minute!" the big man bristled. "If you got yourself shot it wasn't my doing."

John glared at Kramer. "Don't try to tell me that! I checked it out. I know where you went and who the cattle were sold to. So don't try to tell me any different!"

"Those are fighting words, Breckenridge!" Kramer blustered, his hand hovering over the pistol strapped to his hip. "I never stole anything in my life! And anyone who says I did is a liar!"

The marshal remained silent, his own hand close to the handle of his hog-leg.

It was a tense moment, fraught with danger. Both men were teetering on the brink of a show-down. The young marshal fought against the storm that raged within him—the burning demand for revenge. And Kramer was a proud and arrogant man. He would not back down. He would die first. Yet surprisingly, the muscles in his face loosened suddenly and he managed a faint smile.

"I don't blame you for getting your back up," he said, quietly. "I heard somebody hit the herd and you and that crooked gambler lost your beeves and most of your men. I even heard you'd been shot and killed."

"Just shot," John corrected him. "In the back!"

"If I'd done it I'd be going for my gun!" Kramer said. "But to tell you the truth, I'm glad I found you!"

"There's no need to set me straight!" John rasped ominously.

"Mind if I have a chair? I'm powerful tired after coming all the way from Denver on the stage."

John gestured toward a chair that leaned precariously in the direction of the office wall. "Go ahead."

The visitor pulled it out and lowered his big frame into it. The weariness seemed to take hold of him anew. "I don't know why I'm wasting my time trying to talk to you. If you won't believe me, I reckon there's nothing I can do about that. But I'm telling the truth! I was going to steal those cattle back. I admit that! Rafferty cheated me—I swear it! I was so mad at that weasel-faced gambler I could've choked him until his eyes popped out!"

Kramer leaned forward earnestly, determined to make John understand. "I had a lot of time to think while we were in jail," Kramer went on. "Like I told you. I never stole anything in my whole life, except maybe a few critters what was running wild. But I figured if I took that herd—even though Rafferty cheated me out of it—I'd be running from the law for the rest of my life. I didn't want that.

"So when we got out, Jake and I went one

way and Gilson and Murray went the other. I never saw them again until I was putting another herd together down in Texas and they showed up wanting work." He paused. "They'd been in my outfit during the war so I took 'em on. That was the biggest mistake I ever made." He nodded and repeated the statement. "It was, for a fact."

John studied the other man's muscular features. Kramer sounded convincing. He had to give him credit for that. But he couldn't accept all that talk about being innocent. His former partner had some reason for wanting to make him think he hadn't been involved in the raid on the herd.

John eyed the older man. "You don't expect me to accept that!"

A thin smile lifted one corner of Kramer's mouth. "I wish you'd believe me," he said, "but it doesn't make a whole lot of difference one way or the other. You ain't got proof that I stole your cattle or had anything to do with it. And, you're a lawman now. You can't take things into your own hands."

Breckenridge moved closer. "I'm the law here," he rasped, "and I'm supposed to uphold it, but I lost some good friends in that raid. Some mighty good friends. Don't push me or I might forget what I'm supposed to do."

Kramer's heavy features darkened and anger rasped in his throat. "I just came in for a little information. Give it to me and I'll be on my way. You seen them two drovers who used to work for me?"

"Who're you talking about?"

"Emil Gilson and Bull Murray. I've combed Kansas and the Colorado Territory for them, but haven't been able to find hide nor hair of 'em."

194

Breckenridge felt the color creep into his cheeks.

Kramer leaned back in his chair and crossed his legs, ignoring the animosity the marshal revealed. "I managed to get money enough together to take another herd to Montana last summer. It wasn't as big as the one I had two years ago, but it was a start. I was looking to work my way back.

"And everything went all right for a change. We got ourselves up to Montana without any trouble. I got a good price for the cattle and thought everything was going to be fine until I went out on the town with Gilson and Murray. When I finally sobered up I didn't have any money and those two weren't anywhere around." He paused. "You sure you ain't seen them? Pinkerton's traced them to Denver and out of Denver heading this way before they lost track of them. They should've come through here."

John listened without comment.

Kramer got to his feet and prepared to leave. "I don't know what to make of it." He sighed. "I'll probably stay around a couple of days just in case they do show."

He started out the door but came back.

"You ain't happened to see Rafferty lately?"

"Not since I was up Ogallala way."

Kramer laughed. "I suppose I was imagining things, but I thought I saw him a couple of times lately. Had the idea he might be following me."

"He's got good reason to."

"If you see him and he's got any quarrel with me, tell him to face me. It makes a feller powerful uneasy having somebody sneak around behind his back."

John's voice tightened. "You should've

thought of that before you rustled those cows."

"Well, I'm not losing any sleep over him." He laughed curtly. "I'll let you know when I'm going to leave town."

"You do that."

John watched him go, closing the door after him against the winter cold.

Kramer hadn't been gone an hour when he came striding back again. "Just thought I'd tell you I was checking around town when the depot agent caught me. He had a message from Pinkerton's saying Gilson and Murray are in jail in Rapid City. I'm heading there on the next stage. I forgot something. If I do have the wrong info and they come here, throw them in jail. There's a warrant for their arrest. I swore it out myself." He fished two dog-eared posters from his inside coat pocket and handed it to John. "These're all over Denver and half of Colorado."

John studied them. There was no doubt about it. Gilson and Murray were wanted by the Denver authorities for robbery. There was a thousand dollar reward for their arrest.

The young marshal watched as the door slammed shut and he heard the clatter of spurs and hard heels on the boardwalk as Kramer strode purposefully in the direction of the hotel where the stage always stopped. He turned to the work on his desk, but his mind wouldn't settle to it.

After a time he put the books away, closed the damper on the stove, and locked up. He planned on going home when he left the office, but Kramer's questions about Rafferty changed things. If the gambler was trailing Kramer, he would strike soon. A straightforward shootout was one thing. Rafferty had no use for Kramer, but Breckenridge couldn't stand by and see him shot without a chance to defend himself.

John left the office and made the rounds of the saloons, checking to see if any new gamblers had come in looking for a place to work the last two or three days. But no one had seen or talked to anyone resembling Rafferty. John mounted the line-back dun and started home when he changed his mind and went to the hotel. No one by the gambler's description had registered there.

"Have you checked over at the boarding house?" the hotel clerk asked. "There was a feller in here last night who might be your man. Said he couldn't pay a dollar a day for a room so I sent him over there."

John thanked him and went to Martha Lane's Boarding House not far from the church.

"I've had no one by the name of Rafferty," Martha said. "The only new man is Mr. Sanford. He came in last night. Said he would be staying a few days."

John went into the parlor of the big house. The furniture was old and well worn. The paper on the walls was cracked and showing evidence of peeling, and the rug on the floor was bare in spots.

Martha pushed her hair back from the side of her face with a weary hand and called to her ten-year-old son.

"Go up and get Mr. Sanford. Tell him there's someone to see him."

The gambler came down the stairs warily, his hand close to the derringer he always carried. "I heard tell you were the marshal here."

"I want to talk to you, Sam."

197

"I was fixing to see you soon as I had time."

They went back up the stairs and into his scantily furnished room. There was a small grate in the floor that was supposed to let heat up to his room, but it was cold and the frost had gathered on the window.

"Kramer was in to see me today. He says you've been following him. If you've got anything to talk to him about, do it, but don't sneak around or you'll have to answer to me."

The gambler shook his head in disbelief. "You're talking about the man who killed our drovers and stole our herd. I've been trailing him! I admit it! You're the marshal! We can take him now, John! We can make him pay!"

Breckenridge's expression did not change.

"If Kramer gets shot in the back, I'm coming after you!"

"Don't you see? This is our chance!"

"Remember what I said!"

With that John stormed down the stairs and out the door. He had to keep Rafferty from dry-gulching Kramer and he had to find Gilson and Murray and hold them in jail until his former partner got back.

Helen was waiting for him when he got home. She saw the concern in his face and asked about it, but he made no attempt to explain.

"I've got an errand to run out to the Circle R," he said. "I was going tonight, but it's so late I think I'll wait until morning."

She came over and sat on the arm of his chair, looping an arm about his shoulder. "Is there something wrong, John?" she asked.

He managed a thin, tight smile. "It's just police business. A couple of guys who are wanted for

198

robbery are supposed to be out to the Circle R looking for work. I thought I'd check on them."

He planned on leaving Cottonwood for the ranch at first light but he was called to the Lucky Dollar for a fight after supper and he had to lock the men up. That meant Helen had to fix breakfast for them and he had to take it to the jail before he could leave.

By then there was other business to attend to. A saddle bum had frozen to death in the little shed behind Kellerman's store and he had to look into that before turning the body to the undertaker. Then someone had stolen two handguns and a quantity of ammunition from the general store. That investigation took more time. When he finally was able to leave it was after one o'clock.

The clouds were gone and the winter sun was glistening off the snow-covered prairies. A prairie chicken exploded out of a thicket along the road and Breckenridge saw a coyote slinking along the edge of a snowbank, his quarry a jackrabbit too young to be careful. He watched as the predator crept closer and pounced on the unsuspecting little animal.

That was what he hoped to do with Gilson and Murray. Slip into the ranch as quietly as possible and grab them before they had a chance to run.

It was a long, cold ride. He hunched lower in his heavy coat and urged the dun into a trot. It wasn't difficult keeping the big horse on the move in such weather. The gelding sensed that the sooner they reached their destination, the sooner he'd be out of the cold. He stepped out at a fast, distance-eating pace.

Nevertheless, it was after four o'clock when Breckenridge reached the Circle R and talked to the foreman about the two wanted men.

"Haven't seen anybody fittin' those descriptions," he said.

"They told me they were coming out here," Breckenridge repeated. "Said they heard you was hiring."

"We haven't put a new man on for the past five months. If we're lucky enough to keep from gettin' anybody hurt and no one quits, we might get by without any new help—even next summer."

"They left town headed this direction. And I don't know why they'd lie about coming here. It doesn't make good sense."

The foreman pursed his lips. "If you don't mind my saying so, Marshal, I'm surprised you'd come sashaying way out here when the payroll for the mine is coming in tomorrow."

"Tomorrow?" he echoed. "Nobody told me about that."

"I've been watching that stage for the last couple of years—ever since the mine opened. When there are two men riding shotgun like there was this morning they're bringing in the payroll the next day."

"I checked with Parker before I left town," he said. "He didn't say anything about the payroll."

John glanced at his watch and up at the sky. In less than an hour it would be pitch dark. It would be better to stay at the ranch and get up early the next morning and make the long, cold ride. Then both he and his mount would be fresh.

He watered his mount and took him into the barn where he fed and curried him. By the time he went to the house the foreman and the hands were waiting supper on him.

Breckenridge remained silent and the table conversation drifted to the storm and the job of caring for cattle in such weather. They asked how the people in town were managing in the snow and if he had heard any other stories of ranches losing cattle. He answered their questions and offered certain observations of his own.

After supper the men began to drift back to the bunkhouse by ones and twos. John would have joined them, but the foreman insisted that he come into the living room and visit. They didn't often have an overnight guest. It had been months since he and his wife had gone to town, and they were both hungry for someone new to talk to.

It was after ten o'clock when he finally went back to the bunkhouse. He was tired and wanted to sleep, but could say nothing to stop the desultory poker game that was being played on the bunk next to the one assigned to him. Such criticism wouldn't be polite. He went to bed and tried to close his eyes and ears to the noise of the game.

"Want in, Pete?" the dealer asked one of the hands as he shuffled the cards.

"Not me. That feller who was here two or three nights ago plumb cleaned me out. I ain't even got money for smokin' tobacco till payday."

John sat upright. "You wouldn't be talking about a guy by the name of Sanford?"

"You know him?"

"I know him."

"He's a shyster!" Pete exploded. "I knew he was cheating, but he was so slick I couldn't catch him at it."

Breckenridge lay back down and closed his eyes. First Gilson and Murray came to Cottonwood, then Kramer. Now Raffety, bent on revenge had showed up at the Circle R. He didn't know what to make of it, but it meant trouble.

The next morning as soon as they had finished breakfast he saddled the dun and rode off, bracing himself against the subzero weather that had moved in with the darkness of the night before. The wheel tracks were plainly legible. He kept looking for other signs that would indicate the stage was being followed, but if there were any, he hadn't been able to find them.

When he reached the way station he talked with Con Raymond and the hostler who changed teams for them. Raymond's wife was inside. She saw to it that there were meals for the passengers and a spot of coffee if they wanted it—which they usually did.

"Over at the Circle R they told me there's to be a shipment of money on today's stage," he began.

"Money?" Raymond echoed curiously.

"To pay the workers at the Silver Slipper Mine."

"Not today."

Breckenridge frowned. "There were two men riding shotgun on yesterday's Wimberly stage," he explained. "The way I understand it, the only time that happens is when they send guards out so they can guard the mine payroll on the way back."

The stationmaster laughed. "That's usually the case, but we've got us a real, live dignitary on today's stage. A senator, no less." His round face broke into a wide grin. "They sent out word that the senator's wife was concerned about Indian raids and he wanted extra protection." Raymond

202

seemed to feel that eliminated the danger.

John wasn't so sure. If bandits knew the stage carried the payroll every month, they might see the double guard and make the same mistake the foreman at the Circle R had made. "Think I'll stick around and go back to town with the stage," he said.

Raymond went inside and Breckenridge led his mount to the water trough. The hostler came out and offered to take care of it for him, but he usually cared for his horse himself.

"I'm Jimmy Garrison, Mr. Marshal," the young man said. "If you need anything, just call on me. I like to help the law! I surely do." He turned away but came back. "My ma calls me James," he said, "but I don't like that. Everybody else calls me Jimmy. It's, 'Hey, Jimmy, get them horses up here on the double! It's time for the stage!' And 'Jimmy, help this gentleman with his bags.' And 'Jimmy, you take good care of them horses!' I know how to take care of horses good. I ain't had much schoolin'. I can't learn very well. But I know about horses! Ain't nobody in these parts knows horses better than me."

"I'll remember that," John said.

"You'll find out how good I am with horses, Mr. Marshal. You'll see."

The dun finished drinking and John was almost back to the barn with him when the stage rumbled into the yard. Breckenridge eyed the passengers as they got off. The first was a rotund, well-dressed gentleman whose expensive suit was badly soiled and unpressed, mute evidence that he had traveled a long way without a change of clothes. That would be the senator.

A woman about the same age or a little younger climbed down. She would be the senator's wife. She was in a fancy dress with ruffles at the neck and at the wrists. The sleeves billowed out in a fancy way that gave them a special name that he could never remember. And there were ruffles at the hemline of her skirt. It was as dirty and wrinkled as her husband's suit. They surely had duded up clothes for riding a stage.

Then the door opened once more and a big man climbed down. Kramer! He hadn't gone to Rapid; he hadn't even left the area! He had lied about that!

John caught his breath sharply. He didn't know why Kramer was coming in on the stage, especially after saying he was on his way to the Black Hills. But whatever it was, it spelled *trouble!*

22

Kramer had never intended to leave the Colorado foothills. All that talk had been a blind—a smoke-screen to hide the real purpose for coming to Cottonwood. It had to be the payroll that brought him. Whoever gave him information told him about two guards going out on the Wimberly stage, and like everyone else, he decided that the next day's stage would have the payroll. The chances were that Gilson and Murray were in on the deal with him, which could account for Kramer's interest in finding them.

John moved back into the shadows as Kramer turned to say something to the senator's wife. If only he knew when and where the outlaws planned to hit the stage. They might try to hold up the way station while the hostler was changing teams and the passengers were getting a little relief from the grueling ride. Or they might decide to wait until the coach was on the road, beyond the help of Con Raymond and Jimmy.

Without the senator and his wife to be concerned about, he could wait until the bandits struck, making his own move after they were committed. But he had to see that the passengers weren't aboard when the stage left for Cottonwood.

John led the big dun farther into the barn and tied the reins to a manger, his thoughts still on the situation at hand. The matter was solved when Jimmy came out to the barn leading the lathered horses that had just been unhitched from the stage.

"I didn't tell anybody you were out here, Mr. Marshal," he said. "I figured you didn't want anybody to know so I says to myself, 'Jimmy, don't you give the marshal away. If you do, he might be awful mad. And you don't want him mad at you.'"

"You did real good keeping it a secret," John assured him. "Now, I've got something else I need you to help me with." He lowered his voice to impress upon the hostler the urgency of keeping the information quiet.

"This is very important, Jimmy," he continued softly. "I want you to get Con away from the others. Tell him I'm afraid somebody might try to rob the stage here or on the way to Cottonwood."

The boy's eyes rounded and his words were hushed with emotion. "Is that for real?"

"I don't want the senator and his wife to get hurt, so they shouldn't go into Cottonwood on the stage. Have them wait here until we can send them in some other way."

Jimmy nodded emphatically. He had never felt as important as he did right then. The marshal was trusting him with a serious message. That didn't happen every day. "We don't want them to get hurt. They're very important people, ain't they, Mr. Marshal?"

"They certainly are."

The hostler hesitated, going over his instructions in his mind. "You want me to tell Mr. Raymond not to let the senator and his wife get hurt?"

"No, I want you to tell Mr. Raymond not to let the senator and his wife go out on the stage. We'll have to get them to Cottonwood another way."

Jimmy repeated the instructions twice to be sure he had them exactly right.

"And don't let anybody hear you," Breckenridge warned.

Jimmy finished unharnessing the horses, glanced at John for assurance, and dashed for the way station. "Hey, Mr. Raymond!" he shouted when he was fifteen feet from the door. "Mr. Raymond! I've got to talk to you all by yourself. The marshal says the stage is going to be robbed and nobody should go on it! They're going to rob the stage, Mr. Raymond!"

John groaned as the hostler's voice drifted back to him. He drew his gun and looked quickly about the barn, concerned that someone might be hiding there.

The makeshift building was small, without a haymow and with rough board stalls for the horses. Satisfied that it was empty, he moved forward cautiously, examining the area around the buildings. There had been no one in the barn, and he saw no one outside.

It wouldn't be an easy place to approach without being detected, but there was always a way. The prairie stretched endlessly to the far horizon in every direction. There was a stand of cottonwoods and willows and brush of several varieties on the far side of the way station. Men could easily hide there.

He moved slowly through the snow, his hand

on his weapon. His gaze swept the way station carefully for some sign that the bandits were lying in wait.

He was at the water trough when the way station door opened and Kramer came out. His former partner moved with the same caution—slowly, deliberately, his hand never far from his weapon—one measured step at a time. "You lied to me, John," he said reproachfully. "You told me you hadn't seen Gilson and Murray."

John stopped, his feet slightly apart and his eyes narrowing. "I didn't lie. I just didn't answer you."

"You and me were partners once. I was sure that would count for something. Why didn't you tell me?"

"I didn't trust you, Kramer. I still don't."

His former partner winced, or pretended to.

John breathed deeply. "That was a short trip you made to Rapid."

Kramer nodded. "I started. That's a fact. But I got wind those two were in these parts so I came back."

"That was right thoughtful of you."

"And it looks like it's a good thing I'm here. I've got a hunch Gilson and Murray know about the stage and the two guards riding shotgun and figure the payroll's going to move today."

"Could be," John said laconically.

"'Pears to me you're going to need all the help you can get."

"I ain't so sure you're here to help!"

Kramer's lips tightened. "What do you mean by that?" he snarled, his hand drifting towards the butt of his gun.

John caught the ominous warning in his voice

and the sly movement of his hand. "Take it any way you want."

"You're mighty big for your britches."

Kramer went for his gun. The big weapon came up smoothly and he squeezed the trigger. The instant the big man made his move John dove to one side, firing as he went down. The .44 slug tore away the gun and half of Kramer's hand. He bellowed with pain and rage. An instant later his body jerked violently and he lay quite still in the wind-packed snow.

The sound of the first gun triggered a barrage of bullets, coming from either side of the way station. They ripped into the drifted snow around Breckenridge and splintered the top of the wooden water trough he was crouched behind.

Just as Breckenridge suspected, Murray and Gilson were there! Bull appeared from behind the way station, bent over and running hard, his six-gun in his massive hand. He rounded the corner of the building, dashed to the door, and kicked it in. He got off a shot before the marshal fired.

But somebody from inside beat him to it! The report sounded an instant before John's. Murray staggered backwards, swayed like a tree cut off at the roots, and collapsed, crashing to the hard, snow-packed ground.

For an instant all was quiet, save for the mournful soughing of the wind as it swept over the drifts. John raised himself on one knee, cautiously, and studied the sod building and the surrounding area. While he watched, the door creaked open slowly and one of the guards stepped out with his rifle at the ready.

The sudden sound startled someone crouched close to the way station. Whoever it was stepped backward, stumbling in the snow.

"Stop right where you are!" John shouted. "You're under arrest!"

For answer the stranger got off a shot in his direction—a wild, poorly aimed round that went six inches over his head. The outlaw turned and ran.

"Stop!" the officer ordered again, scrambling after the desperado.

But whoever it was had no intention of stopping. He dashed to his horse, loosed the reins, and jumped into the saddle, whirling to fire once more. This time the shot went to one side.

John squeezed the trigger and the highwayman pitched forward, sprawling in the snow. Only then did he see that it was Rafferty, lying face down!

The brief battle wasn't quite over. Gilson came around the other side of the little building. Seeing his partner on the reddening snow stopped him. Briefly he stared down at Murray, then brought his revolver up and was about to fire when the guard still inside shot twice. Gilson went down beside his friend.

John started forward, but Con Raymond and one of the guards came out of the way station, checked the bodies nearest the door, and went on to where Rafferty was lying. Breckenridge went up to Kramer, who opened his eyes.

"I should've known better than to try to outgun you," he mumbled.

John knelt beside him. "Let's have a look at that hand."

The injured man glared at him but was silent while he examined the wound.

"I see you found Murray and Gilson," John said.

"You ain't surprised, are you?"

"I figured whatever brought you here included those two."

Kramer's eyes rolled in pain, and it was a moment or two before he could go on. "They were the ones who found out about you being marshal in Cottonwood. I wasn't that keen on tangling with you again, but they talked me into it. Said we could knock off one of the biggest payrolls in Colorado and get back at you at the same time. Only it didn't work out that way."

"They were with you when you stole our herd, weren't they?"

Kramer tried to move and groaned audibly. "They've been with me since the war. Stayed by me when hardly nobody else did. I never forgot that!"

"John!" Raymond called from the place where Rafferty was lying. "This man's dying and wants to talk to you!"

By this time the senator and his wife were with Kramer.

"There isn't much anybody can do for his hand," Breckenridge said.

She examined the wounded man competently. "It isn't his hand we're worried about," she retorted. "He's been shot in the back. And it's bad!"

John stared at her incredulously. He couldn't have hit Kramer in the back even if he'd wanted to.

"Hurry," the stationmaster repeated. "He's not going to last long!"

The marshal left Kramer and walked through the snow to the spot where Rafferty was lying in a widening pool of blood. Raymond and the guard were bending over him.

"I–I didn't think you'd do it," the wounded man said to John haltingly. "Kramer stole your herd, too. I figured you were on my side!"

"I tried to tell you. I'm on the side of the law!"

By this time the way station had emptied and the men crowded around the marshal and the dying gambler.

"I've seen him before!" the driver exclaimed. "He was nosing around the station at Wimberly."

Rafferty's breath was coming in long, gurgling gasps and it was all he could do to force out the words. "But I got him!" he managed triumphantly. "All I had to do was follow Gilson and Murray. I knew they were up to something and I was sure Kramer was in on it. But I got him." He swore savagely.

"What do you mean?"

"You don't think that hand shot of yours killed him, do you? I said I'd get even and I did!" He closed his eyes for a minute or more.

"Think we ought to do try to do something for him?" the stationmaster asked.

"Ain't no use," the driver put in. "He's bought the farm."

But Rafferty was not dead yet. "I want you to know something else, Breckenridge," he rasped, his voice little more than a tortured whisper. "I was after you, too! I got you in the back during the cattle raid. Only I didn't do as good a job on you as I did on Kramer just now! I should've knocked you off for good, but with all them bullets flyin' around I didn't take time to shoot straight."

"So it wasn't Kramer who shot me after all!"

"Maybe he should've. He'd have done it right!" The effort of speaking seemed too much for him. He closed his eyes and the men around him were certain that he had breathed his last. Then his body jerked spasmodically and his neck relaxed, allowing his head to turn to one side.

The senator touched Breckenridge on the shoulder. "I want to thank you for what you did," he said. "You tipped their hand and made them try to take us here. We don't know what would have happened if they'd followed us and hit us on the road." His voice was somber. "We might have been the ones who'd be lying—"

"I'm getting cold, Mr. Marshal," Jimmy broke in suddenly. "Can't we go in?"

"You go ahead, Jimmy. We'll get the bodies wrapped up and on top of the stage. Then we'll all go in and get warm before starting for Cotton-wood."

Still the hostler did not move. "Mr. Marshal," he said, "I did good telling Con to keep Mr. and Mrs. Senator from being on the stage, didn't I? Didn't I?"

He grinned at him. "Yes, Jimmy. The way it worked out you did real good."

John went back to Kramer, but the senator's wife had just turned away. "He's dead!" she choked.

"And so are the others," Jimmy added. "All of them!"

The stage was two hours late getting in to Cottonwood Springs and the people in town were sure something had happened. They were form-ing a posse to go out and see when the driver

213

brought the team down main street at a dead run. A dozen people braved the cold to come out and see what had happened.

"We had a little problem at the way station," the senator informed them, "but everything worked out."

Kellerman approached the politician's wife. "Are you sure you're all right?"

"Quite," she said, smiling.

John made arrangements with the undertaker to bury the outlaws and answered a few questions thrown at him by the town officials. When that was over he mounted and rode home. Helen was worried about him.

"Mrs. Kellerman was here," she said. "The men were concerned enough to get a posse together. They were going to ride out to see what was wrong."

He pulled out a chair and sat down wearily at the kitchen table. She brought him a steaming cup of coffee and he sipped it gratefully.

A peace that he hadn't had in months swept over him. He hadn't killed Kramer. He hadn't even shot at him in anger. He shot him in the hand because his former partner fired first.

What if he had goaded Kramer into a fight and killed him for revenge, when Kramer wasn't even guilty of the shooting? Kramer had been responsible for stealing the herd, that was true. But he hadn't shot John. What if he had killed Kramer in revenge and then had learned that Rafferty was guilty? He would be the one to agonize over what had happened. He had been spared that. He hadn't even killed Rafferty in revenge. He fired at him as the marshal and because the gambler fired first.

Helen saw the look on his face and smiled. "It's so nice to see you like this," she said. "You look happy."

"I am," he answered. "Happier than I've been in a long time."

OTHER WESTERNS from Living Books

Westerns in the Living Books series feature the action and excitement you expect from Westerns—plus a concern for moral choices and personal integrity. In the great tradition of American Western novels, Living Books offers you quality stories that show—with realism and compassion—the age-old conflict between good and evil.

THE DRIFTER by Gilbert Morris. War-weary drifter Jim Reno finds himself caught in the conflict between the greedy Carrs of Skull Ranch and a group of small ranchers. Though tired of violence, Reno is determined to free the ranchers from Skull's exploitation. Number 1 in the Reno Westerns Series.

TREACHERY AT CIMARRON by Jim Ross. Ruthless killers and a beautiful scheming woman haunt the Cimarron range, seeking a rancher's gold. Marks Dunlee learns of the plot and plans a daring rescue. Number 1 in the Dunlee Westerns Series.

AMBUSH AT VERMEJO by Jim Ross. Lonan Dunlee sees a rancher ambushed and vows to find the killers. In the search he unravels an elaborate scheme involving a false burial, a conniving brother, a corrupt lawman, and the vicious Gaster brothers. Number 2 in the Dunlee Westerns Series.

BRECK'S CHOICE by Bernard Palmer. Former gunman John Breck had sworn never to use a gun again. But when his gold is stolen and his wife and child are murdered, he must find the killers. And his only clue is a broken hoofprint. Number 1 in the Breck Westerns Series.

HUNTED GUN by Bernard Palmer. Colorado rancher John Breck encounters an ambush, suspicious townspeople, and deceit spawned by gold fever as he searches for the killers of a rancher who just found gold. Number 2 in the Breck Westerns Series.

KID BRECKINRIDGE by Bernard Palmer. This tale introduces young John Breckinridge (the John Breck of *Breck's Choice* and *Hunted Gun*). John, a runaway, learns a lot about the Old West as he experiences an Indian ambush, a cattle drive, and a bank robbery. Number 3 in the Breck Westerns Series.

Other Living Books Best-sellers

THE ANGEL OF HIS PRESENCE by Grace Livingston Hill. This book captures the romance of John Wentworth Stanley and a beautiful young woman whose influence causes John to reevaluate his well-laid plans for the future. 07-0047 $2.50.

HOW TO BE HAPPY THOUGH MARRIED by Tim LaHaye. One of America's most successful marriage counselors gives practical, proven advice for marital happiness. 07-1499 $3.50.

JOHN, SON OF THUNDER by Ellen Gunderson Traylor. In this saga of adventure, romance, and discovery, travel with John—the disciple whom Jesus loved—down desert paths, through the courts of the Holy City, to the foot of the cross. Journey with him from his luxury as a privileged son of Israel to the bitter hardship of his exile on Patmos. 07-1903 $4.95.

KAREN'S CHOICE by Janice Hermansen. College students Karen and Jon fall in love and are heading toward marriage when Karen discovers she is pregnant. Struggle with Karen and Jon through the choices they make and observe how they cope with the consequences and eventually find the forgiveness of Christ. 07-2027 $3.50.

LIFE IS TREMENDOUS! by Charlie "Tremendous" Jones. Believing that enthusiasm makes the difference, Jones shows how anyone can be happy, involved, relevant, productive, healthy, and secure in the midst of a high-pressure, commercialized society. 07-2184 $2.50.

LOOKING FOR LOVE IN ALL THE WRONG PLACES by Joe White. Using wisdom gained from many talks with young people, White steers teens in the right direction to find love and fulfillment in a personal relationship with God. 07-3825 $3.50.

LORD, I KEEP RUNNING BACK TO YOU by Ruth Harms Calkin. In prayer-poems tinged with wonder, joy, humanness, and questioning, the author speaks for all of us who are groping and learning together what it means to be God's child. 07-3819 $3.50.

SUCCESS: THE GLENN BLAND METHOD by Glenn Bland. The author shows how to set goals and make plans that really work. His ingredients of success include spiritual, financial, educational, and recreational balances. 07-6689 $3.50.

MOUNTAINS OF SPICES by Hannah Hurnard. Here is an allegory comparing the nine spices mentioned in the Song of Solomon to the nine fruits of the Spirit. A story of the glory of surrender by the author of *HINDS' FEET ON HIGH PLACES.* 07-4611 $3.50.

THE NEW MOTHER'S BOOK OF BABY CARE by Marjorie Palmer and Ethel Bowman. From what you will need to clothe the baby to how to know when to call the doctor, this book will give you all the basic knowledge necessary to be the parent your child needs. 07-4695 $2.95.

Other Living Books Best-sellers

ANSWERS by Josh McDowell and Don Stewart. In a question-and-answer format, the authors tackle sixty-five of the most-asked questions about the Bible, God, Jesus Christ, miracles, other religions, and creation.   07-0021 $3.95.

THE BEST CHRISTMAS PAGEANT EVER by Barbara Robinson. A delightfully wild and funny story about what happens to a Christmas program when the "Horrible Herdman" brothers and sisters are miscast in the roles of the biblical Christmas story characters.   07-0137 $2.50.

BUILDING YOUR SELF-IMAGE by Josh McDowell. Here are practical answers to help you overcome your fears, anxieties, and lack of self-confidence. Learn how God's higher image of who you are can take root in your heart and mind.   07-1395 $3.95.

THE CHILD WITHIN by Mari Hanes. The author shares insights she gained from God's Word during her own pregnancy. She identifies areas of stress, offers concrete data about the birth process, and points to God's sure promises that he will "gently lead those that are with young."   07-0219 $2.95.

400 WAYS TO SAY I LOVE YOU by Alice Chapin. Perhaps the flame of love has almost died in your marriage. Maybe you have a good marriage that just needs a little "spark." Here is a book especially for the woman who wants to rekindle the flame of romance in her marriage; who wants creative, practical, useful ideas to show the man in her life that she cares.   07-0919 $2.50.

GIVERS, TAKERS, AND OTHER KINDS OF LOVERS by Josh McDowell and Paul Lewis. This book bypasses vague generalities about love and sex and gets right to the basic questions: Whatever happened to sexual freedom? What's true love like? Do men respond differently than women? If you're looking for straight answers about God's plan for love and sexuality, this book was written for you.   07-1031 $2.95.

HINDS' FEET ON HIGH PLACES by Hannah Hurnard. A classic allegory of a journey toward faith that has sold more than a million copies!   07-1429 $3.95.

LORD, COULD YOU HURRY A LITTLE? by Ruth Harms Calkin. These prayer-poems from the heart of a godly woman trace the inner workings of the heart, following the rhythms of the day and the seasons of the year with expectation and love.   07-3816 $2.95.

WHAT WIVES WISH THEIR HUSBANDS KNEW ABOUT WOMEN by James Dobson. The best-selling author of *DARE TO DISCIPLINE* and *THE STRONG-WILLED CHILD* brings us this vital book that speaks to the unique emotional needs and aspirations of today's woman. An immensely practical, interesting guide.   07-7896 $3.50.

Other Living Books Best-sellers

LORD, YOU LOVE TO SAY YES by Ruth Harms Calkin. In this collection of prayer-poems the author speaks openly and honestly with her Lord about hopes and dreams, longings and frustrations, and her observations of life. 07-3824 $2.95.

MORE THAN A CARPENTER by Josh McDowell. A hard-hitting book for people who are skeptical about Jesus' deity, his resurrection, and his claims on their lives. 07-4552 $2.95.

NOW IS YOUR TIME TO WIN by Dave Dean. In this true-life story, Dean shares how he locked into seven principles that enabled him to bounce back from failure to success. Read about successful men and women—from sports and entertainment celebrities to the ordinary people next door—and discover how you too can bounce back from failure to success! 07-4727 $2.95.

THE POSITIVE POWER OF JESUS CHRIST by Norman Vincent Peale. All his life the author has been leading men and women to Jesus Christ. In this book he tells of his boyhood encounters with Jesus and of his spiritual growth as he attended seminary and began his world-renowned ministry. 07-4914 $3.95.

REASONS by Josh McDowell and Don Stewart. In a convenient question-and-answer format, the authors address many of the commonly asked questions about the Bible and evolution. 07-5287 $3.95.

ROCK by Bob Larson. A well-researched and penetrating look at today's rock music and rock performers, their lyrics, and their life-styles. 07-5686 $3.50.

SHAPE UP FROM THE INSIDE OUT by John R. Throop. Learn how to conquer the problem of being overweight! In this honest, often humorous book, Throop shares his own personal struggle with this area and how he gained fresh insight about the biblical relationship between physical and spiritual fitness. 07-5899 $2.95.

TAKE ME HOME by Bonnie Jamison. This touching, candid story of the author's relationship with her dying mother will offer hope and assurance to those dealing with an aging parent, relative, or friend. 07-6901 $3.50.

TELL ME AGAIN, LORD, I FORGET by Ruth Harms Calkin. You will easily identify with Calkin in this collection of prayer-poems about the challenges, peaks, and quiet moments of each day. 07-6990 $3.50.

THROUGH GATES OF SPLENDOR by Elisabeth Elliot. This unforgettable story of five men who braved the Auca Indians has become one of the most famous missionary books of all times. 07-7151 $3.95.

WAY BACK IN THE HILLS by James C. Hefley. The story of Hefley's colorful childhood in the Ozarks makes reflective reading for those who like a nostalgic journey into the past. 07-7821 $3.95.

The books listed are available at your bookstore. If unavailable, send check with order to cover retail price plus $1.00 per book for postage and handling to:

Christian Book Service
Box 80
Wheaton, Illinois 60189

Prices and availability subject to change without notice. Allow 4–6 weeks for delivery.